His words refuted what his kiss had implied

In Ross's arms Sharon had just gained an inkling of the explosive forces that could be generated between man and woman.

But when he suddenly thrust her away, Sharon's shock was all the greater for this newfound knowledge.

He snarled, "You like us all, don't you? Steve, my brother, Greg, and me. It's all the same — the token struggle and then the come-on. There's a word for women like you!"

"You're wrong," Sharon stammered, too shocked to be anything but honest. "Ross, it's not like that."

"Spare me the wide-eyed innocence, okay?" he said heavily. "And let's get something straight — if you're going to fool around with my brother again, you won't do it on my property. Do you understand?"

The Tides of Summer

Sandra Field

Harlequin Books

TORONTO • NEW YORK • LONDON
AMSTERDAM • PARIS • SYDNEY • HAMBURG
STOCKHOLM • ATHENS • TOKYO • MILAN

Original hardcover edition published in 1983
by Mills & Boon Limited

ISBN 0-373-02577-7

Harlequin Romance first edition October 1983

For
JANET

CHAPTER ONE

THE wind tugged at the heavy folds of Sharon's poncho, which covered her from head to knee, and pulled wisps of black hair free of her braid, blowing them across her face. Her laden pack gave her a peculiarly hump-backed appearance. She trudged up the hill, feeling the first drops of rain sting her cheeks. The massed clouds that had darkened from grey to purple at the onset of dusk had been warning her of rain; however, she had hoped it might hold off until she was camped for the night. No such luck, she thought ruefully, pulling her hood up over her hair and tying the strings under her chin.

As she topped the rise, there opened in front of her the full vista of smoothly rolling hills, where cleared land and white-painted farmhouses were interspersed with woodlots; the landscape was split by the wide channel of the river, its muddy waters churned by the twin forces of wind and tide. Lights had already been turned on in the scattered houses, and for once Sharon found herself envying the occupants, who were warm and dry and safe. She shivered, lowering her head against the rain and starting down the hill, keeping to the gravelled shoulder of the road rather than the sleek, wet pavement.

That brief reconnaissance on the hilltop had shown her something else: a cluster of lights a couple of miles away signalling one of the small country towns that had been following the course of the river. Maybe she'd dip into her diminishing store of money and stay in a guest house overnight, she thought, with a lift of her spirits. It would be lovely to have a hot bath and sleep in a bed for a change; much better than trying to put up her tent in this wind.

If the truck had not come over the hill then, that was probably what she would have done, and the whole course of her summer—and indeed, of her life—would

7

have been different. But the truck did come over the hill, its springs rattling, its headlights picking out the sexless figure tramping along the edge of the road. The brakes squealed and the truck shuddered to a halt.

Sharon looked up. The driver had leaned over and was winding down the window on her side. 'Want a drive?' he called out.

She hesitated briefly. His voice was rough, his face, what she could see of it, coarsely featured. If she had been in Montreal, she would have said no very politely and kept on her way. But this wasn't Montreal; it was the Annapolis Valley of Nova Scotia, the country, and surely no harm could come to her here? A gust of wind drove a volley of rain against her face, and this decided her. 'Thanks!' she yelled. 'Is there room for my pack in the front?'

'Throw it in the back of the truck.'

She went round to the rear of the vehicle, noticing absently that one of the brake lights was burned out and that the entire back bumper seemed to be rusted through, what was left of it anchored with string. It was not a vehicle to inspire much confidence, she thought, hoping she wasn't taking her life in her hands. She pulled her poncho over her head, undid the nylon straps of her backpack and lifted it over the tailgate of the truck to lie among the clutter of chains, plastic piping, and bags of sawdust. At least the plywood roof would keep it dry.

Clutching her poncho, she ran back to the side of the truck and climbed in. With a squeal of gears the truck moved off down the hill.

'Where're you headin'?'

'I was going to the campground the other side of Woodley, but maybe I'll get you to let me off in the next little town.'

'Lookin' for a place to stay?'

'Yes,' she said warily. Now that she had caught her breath and had had a chance to look a little more closely at her rescuer, she was even less sure about the wisdom of her decision in taking this ride. The hands that gripped the steering wheel had thick wrists and blunt/fingers, the nails grimed with dirt. He did not look much taller than she, but he did look a great deal stronger, his shoulders straining at the seams of a sweat-stained flannel shirt. A cigarette dangled from his lips. He was unshaven.

Sharon was not particularly bothered by his general lack of cleanliness, for she was a practical girl who knew that farmers, particularly in summer, did not have the time or the energy to be overly fastidious about their appearance. It was a looseness in the mouth, a hint of calculation in the light blue eyes when they rested on her, that disturbed her. Unconsciously she moved a little further away from him.

'You from around here?'

'No, I'm not,' she answered shortly.

'On your own?'

'I'm meeting friends later on,' she lied.

'Yeah?' He was plainly not convinced.

They had reached the narrow main street of the little town with its obligatory post office, drug store, and bank, its wooden store fronts. 'Why don't you let me off anywhere around here?' Sharon said steadily. 'You've saved me from getting drenched, and I really appreciate that.'

He did not bother slowing down. 'There's nowhere here for you to stay. I'll take you someplace better.'

'Look, Mr——'

'Steve's the name.' He stubbed out the butt of his cigarette in the already overloaded ashtray.

'Look, Steve, I'd rather get out here.' She tried to speak firmly enough that he would pay heed to her, yet not so firmly as to offend him.

He swung round a corner by a shingled church and plunged down a road that within a few hundred feet became dirt-surfaced. 'When I first saw you, I thought you were a boy,' he remarked, flicking her figure up and down with his eyes. 'Not every day I get to give a ride to a pretty girl.'

She fought back the first nibblings of panic. The houses had thinned out, the road now edged with deep, water-filled ditches, some bordered with trees, others with open fields stretching into the darkness from their high banks. For it was fully dark now, a darkness all the more threatening because of the rain that lashed at the windshield and the wind that rocked the truck. 'Where are we going?' she asked coldly.

'You haven't told me your name yet.' Before she could realize his intention, he reached out with his hand and ran it from her jean-clad knee up her thigh.

Sharon struck his hand away, anger drowning out fear and obliterating caution as well. 'Don't do that!'

'Come off it. A girl out on the road by herself. You're only looking for one thing.'

'As it happens, you're quite wrong. I'm looking for a place to spend the night—and I want to spend it alone.'

'Then you picked the wrong guy. You asked where we're going—we're going to my place.' He hit a series of potholes, and metal banged on metal as the truck shook alarmingly. 'Fifteen miles up the road.'

'You won't get away with this—I'll go to the police!'

'Good luck,' he drawled. 'I got no phone, for one thing. For another, you were hitchhiking——'

'I was not! I didn't ask you to stop.'

'I'll tell them you did. And I'll say you asked to stay at my place because of the rain and all. Wonder who they'll believe?'

Fear took the upper hand again. He sounded so damned sure of himself, and his words had a crazy kind of logic . . . she peered through the glass, her vision distorted by the wipers, as the slow minutes ticked by. No lights in sight at all now. Only the narrow red dirt road, awash with water in places, treacherous with mud in others. She was sitting as far away from him as she could, and with her right hand she felt for the doorhandle on her side of the truck. If only he'd slow down, she'd risk jumping out and being left alone in the middle of nowhere—anything would be better than feeling that coarse hand on her leg again. Almost as if he had read her thoughts, he did shift his foot from the accelerator to the brake and ahead of her in the wavering beam of the headlights she saw a crossroads. No signposts. No houses. But he was slowing down. . . . She braced herself to make a jump for it.

He shoved the brakes to the floor with startling suddenness, flinging her off her perch so that her chest struck the dashboard. Then, like a nightmare from which there is no waking up, she felt his hands seize her and pull her towards him and felt his mouth fasten itself on hers with brutal, sickening strength. Momentarily she was paralysed. It was his hand fumbling through her sweater for her breast that brought her to her senses. Sheer terror giving her a strength she did not know she possessed, she lashed out at him with her boots, raking her fingernails down the side of his face.

At any other time his oath would have made her blush. But all she was aware of was the loosening of his hand. Another vicious kick that caught him on the shinbone. Then she was free, scrambling across the width of the seat, frantically searching for the handle. Her fingers curved around the smooth metal. Jerking the door open, she almost fell out of the truck, hitting the ground with a knee-jarring thud. Without even thinking she ran back the way they had come, leaping the ditch and clambering up the far side on all fours, heedless of the mud and rocks. As they had driven past, she must subconsciously have noticed the trees; now she flung herself into their welcoming shelter, dodging branches and the thick trunks as her eyes adjusted to the darkness, her ears straining for any sounds of pursuit.

Her headlong flight lasted four or five minutes, by which time Sharon was gasping for breath, a sharp pain knifing her chest. Ducking behind an old pine tree, she leaned against the rough bark and tried to fill her lungs with air, the sound of her own heartbeat louder in her ears than the keening of the wind through the boughs of the trees or the dripping of rain from the canopy of branches above her head. She heard no footsteps, no crashing of another body through the woods.

Gradually her breathing steadied, and the fingers that had been digging into the bark loosened their hold. He had not followed her ... thank heavens. Knowing he might be waiting for her at the edge of the woods, she stood for what felt like a very long time in the shelter of the big tree. If it had not been raining, she might have curled up where she was and tried to sleep until daylight. But she was already very wet, and knew she would have to find shelter of some kind. Cautiously she peered around the pine tree in the direction from which she had come.

It was pitch dark. Even so, she was able to distinguish the straight black columns of the tree trunks and the blacker solidity of the ground as well as the frenzied dance of the boughs to the wind's wild music. There was no sign of Steve.

She stepped out from behind the tree, every nerve on edge, stifling a scream as a branch tapped at her shoulder. If she could not see him, she thought stoutly, then equally he could not see her. She took a half dozen more steps.

Far ahead of her through the trees a glow of light suddenly sprang to life. As she stood rooted to the ground, Sharon's initial, panic-stricken reaction was that Steve was coming after her with a flashlight. Then common sense reasserted itself. The light was both too bright and too diffuse for that. It could only be the headlights of the truck. To prove her right, the light began to move away from her, and distantly, over the wind, came the growl of an engine.

Transfixed with relief, she watched the light become dimmer and dimmer, then disappear altogether, swallowed up by the inky blackness of the night. Gone . . . he was gone.

With more confidence she began threading her way through the trees towards the road; as she grew nearer, the rush of water in the ditch grew louder. About to step into the open, she suddenly froze to stillness as it occurred to her that he might be trying to trick her: he might have turned on the lights and driven for a few yards to make her believe he had gone. Whereas in reality he would be sitting and waiting for her to emerge on to the road.

Moving as unobtrusively as she could, she started walking parallel to the road, always sheltered by the trees. Within only a minute or two she came to the crossroads. As far as she could see in any direction, there was no sign of the truck. In a spurt of defiance she slid down the embankment and jumped over the ditch, climbing back on to the road. Nothing. No truck, and not a light in sight. Nor could she see either her backpack or her poncho, she thought grimly, adding thief to her list of epithets for the absent Steve. About the only comfort she had was that her thin wad of traveller's cheques was in the back pocket of her jeans, rather than in her pack.

She had no idea which way he had gone. Making a snap decision with no particular reasoning behind it, she turned right and began to walk down the middle of the road, her hands in her pockets, her head downbent.

The wind was behind her; perhaps that had been why, instinctively, she had chosen this direction, she thought wryly. But in no time the rain had penetrated her Lopi sweater and her jeans, soaking through to her skin, making the fabric cling wetly to her body. She increased her pace to try and keep warm, purposely concentrating on the effort of putting one foot in front of the other. It was useless to fret over what the next two or three hours might bring; to keep moving became her only aim.

She walked for perhaps an hour, the last fifteen minutes being steadily uphill, until her legs were aching and her whole body chilled through despite the exercise. The rain had settled into a drenching downpour, although the wind did seem to have abated somewhat. But when she finally reached the crest of the hill, there was a new wind blowing against her face, carrying with it, intangibly, the faraway tang of the sea.

Her vision had long ago completely adjusted to the darkness. In front of her the road sloped downwards to what seemed to be a vast expanse of flat meadowland. But it was not that that held her eye. At the foot of the slope appeared to be a small cluster of buildings, and like beacons in the night three lights shone bravely through the darkness. Lights meant people, she thought in a rush of relief that left her weak at the knees; and people meant food and warmth and shelter.

The farm, if it was a farm, was a deceptively long distance away, for the road twisted and turned on its way to its destination, the water in the ditches following it blindly, tumbling and splashing as it went. But finally she crossed a railway track, a reassuringly civilised sight, and as the road curved to the right she saw that the lights were indeed those of a farm. The first was on a long low building covered with aluminium siding; the second on a more traditional barn with weathered grey shingles and a high-angled roof topped with a weathervane; the third on a two-storied, cedar-shingled house with square-paned windows and a white-painted door. But all the windows in the house were darkened; the place could have been deserted.

Sharon had no idea how much time had elapsed since Steve had picked her up, but she had a feeling it was still before midnight—surely rather early for everyone to have gone to bed?

She was closer now, able to distinguish on her right the regular rows of what must be an orchard, on her left a neat white fence running along the edge of the road; to her nostrils drifted the mingled aroma of manure and wet grass. A gap in the fence signalled the driveway. A sign was creaking in the wind, black letters on white. 'Marshwinds Farm', it said.

She hesitated only briefly, for she could see no other houses farther along the road and not for anything would she have turned around and gone back the way she had come. Turning into the driveway, feeling like an interloper, she began to walk towards the house. She could distinguish other smaller buildings now, more like sheds or garages. The aluminium barn she ignored; it appeared to be totally closed up, something unwelcoming in its blank metal walls. But on the sheltered side of the second barn, under the light, a small door stood open, a black rectangle that nevertheless beckoned to her as representing at the very least a shelter from the rain. Trying not to slip on the mud, she went closer to it. There was a single wooden step, worn smooth by the passage of countless feet. She stepped over it.

Inside, her nostrils were of more use to her than her

eyes, for the outdoor light had temporarily blinded her. The dusty, dry air was redolent with the scent of hay. But there was something else. Somehow she sensed nearby the warm, living presence of animals, cows perhaps, nor was she surprised when she was able to distinguish to her left a narrow flight of descending wooden stairs. There were creatures of some kind down there, she was sure.

Coming in out of the rain seemed only to have made her colder. Gritting her teeth to stop their chattering, she hesitated in the doorway. The house was only a few hundred feet away, and it would be a very simple matter to walk across the grass, knock on the door, and wake someone up. Or would it be that simple? She thought of the inevitable questions, of all the explanations, and her heart quailed.

She looked back over her shoulder into the barn. The hay would be clean and dry—and surely that was a heap of empty feed bags in the corner? She could cover herself with those. In the morning, when the owners of the farm were up and about, she could explain her dilemma far more easily than now, when she would have to rouse them out of bed. And certainly she could do nothing about retrieving her backpack until tomorrow.

The decision made, she walked further into the barn over the uneven floorboards. A lot of the hay was piled up in bales, but some of it was loose as well. She pulled at it, flattening it into a kind of mattress, firmly keeping her mind off the possibility of mice or spiders. Spreading some of the feed sacks flat to lie on, she made a rough pillow out of them and then brought over an armful to use as a blanket. Then she took off her hiking boots and pulled her sweater over her head, leaving on her jeans and a light cotton T-shirt; a change of clothing would have been heaven, but as there was no possibility of it, she tried to forget the discomfort caused by the wet fabric against her skin. Finally she lay down, pulling the coarsely woven bags over her as best she could.

The rain was drumming on the roof. The hay

seemed to be full of mysterious rustlings, the origin of which she did not care to think about. And now that she was lying down, she realised how desperately tired she was. Too tired ... every muscle in her body seemed to be aching, every nerve twitching, and even though she huddled down deep into the hay, it was impossible to get warm or to stop herself from shivering. Besides which, the hay and feed bags were itchy.

She closed her eyes, determined to sleep, hugging her arms across her breast for warmth and curling up her knees. But as the tremors continued to shake her frame and sleep continued to evade her, she could only acknowledge to herself that the worst feeling of all was not the cold or the discomfort, but the loneliness. The sense of being absolutely alone in the dark. At this precise moment in time no one knew where she was: not her friend Joan, who had stood by her through thick and thin during all those dreadful days at the hospital; not Roger, who had not stood by her, but had disassociated himself from the scandal and the gossip; certainly not her unknown grandmother of the beautiful copperplate handwriting and the very definite opinions. No one knew ... and of them all, only Joan would really care.

Physical and emotional exhaustion must eventually have overtaken her. She slept and woke, slept, dreamed, and woke again, stiff and cramped and cold. Then the dream reclaimed her. She was running through the woods, branches like hands with twisted fingers reaching out to grab her, roots writhing up from the ground to trip her, and behind her was the thud of footsteps, growing closer, closer. ... She was jerked awake, her blood congealing in her veins in primitive terror as she heard the footsteps. Heavy. Scraping on the ground. Terrifyingly near. Nightmare had passed into reality, and she was trapped ... a scream burst from her lips as a huge black shape leaped at her across the hay.

Paralysed with fear, dazed and confused, she heard a deep voice order, 'Down, Wolf, down!' Then a light was shining right in her eyes, blindingly bright. In mute protest she covered her eyes with the back of her hand. The same voice, now edged with anger, demanded, 'Who the hell are you? And what are you doing here?'

She lowered her hand, blinking in the light, not sure whether she was trembling from fear or cold or both. The dog who had been so peremptorily spoken to was an immense husky, now sitting obediently at the feet of the man holding the flashlight. Because the man was behind the light, his face was thrown into shadow, his eyes dark sockets, his mouth a thin line.

Totally at a disadvantage, Sharon struggled to a sitting position, pushing damp black tendrils of hair back from her face. 'I was lost,' she stammered. 'There were no lights on in the house, that's why I came in here.'

The beam of the torch left her face to travel over the surrounding hay and the floorboards. 'Are you alone?'

Her throat tightened with panic; it was too uncannily repetitious of Steve's question. She sat up a little straighter, not wanting him to see how frightened she was. 'Yes,' she said baldly.

'I've never seen you before—you don't live around here.'

Once again the flashlight was swung directly at her eyes. It was like an interrogation, she thought, in a spasm of near-hysteria. 'Do you have to do that?' she complained. 'It hurts my eyes.'

He lowered the torch abruptly. 'Sorry. But you haven't answered a single one of my questions. Who are you, and what are you doing here?'

The cool night air struck her bare arms and the damp T-shirt; on the back of her neck her single thick braid of hair lay wet and heavy. She was shivering uncontrollably, her eyes deep pools in a paper-white face. When she spoke, her voice seemed to come from a long way away. 'My name is Sharon Reid,' she said mechanically, too stupefied by everything that had happened to her in the last few hours to produce anything but the truth. 'I'm from Montreal. I was hitchhiking——'

'Where's your gear?' His voice like a whiplash.

She tried to stand up, so at least she could confront

him on more equal terms, but her knees seemed to have lost all their strength. He made no attempt to help her, watching her efforts with a cold-eyed detachment that further eroded her fragile composure. 'It was stolen,' she began.

'A likely story!'

The derisive curl of his lip was the final straw. Her pride in rags, she felt tears crowding her eyes. 'It's true,' she quavered, and then the tears overflowed.

'Oh, for heaven's sake, do you have to cry? That's the oldest trick in the book.' He gave her a look of scalding contempt.

Had he given her sympathy, she would have been crying in earnest. As it was, his contempt miraculously dried her eyes, and from somewhere, she could not have said where, she found the strength to stand up; in her socked feet she was a head shorter than he, and suddenly, recklessly, she couldn't have cared less. 'My pack *was* stolen!' she said with a defiant lift of her chin. 'And if you and the man who stole it are what all the people around here are like, I can't wait to leave here!'

He came a step closer, apparently as unaffected by her rage as he had been by her tears. 'I know your type,' he said coldly. 'You work just long enough to get unemployment and then you take to the roads and live off the people who aren't afraid to do a decent day's work, spinning any kind of a hard luck story that'll get you a free meal——'

Furious, she interrupted him. 'I'm not like that!' Digging in her back pocket, she waved the blue plastic billfold at him. 'I have my own money. And I wouldn't eat at your table if it was the last thing I did!'

As he grabbed her by the arm, his nails digging into her flesh, she realised he had not heard a word she had said. He was in the grip of some violent emotion, far more angry, surely, than he should have been for simply having found an unknown girl half his size in his barn; if ever she had seen murder in a man's eyes, it was in his. 'Let go!' she choked.

If anything, his fingers tightened their hold. His voice harsh with rage, he snarled, 'You're all alike. You drink too much. You sleep around. And you get your kicks with drugs.' He shook her as if she was an animal. 'Don't you?'

The word had struck her like a blow. He couldn't know about her ... he couldn't. 'Drugs?' she faltered, wondering with a strange sort of detachment if she was going to faint.

He shook her again so that her teeth rattled in her head. 'Yes, drugs. So you do know what I'm talking about, don't you? It's written all over you.'

He released her arm so suddenly that she staggered and nearly fell. Then he seized her by the shirt and she heard the fabric tear and felt the bite of his fingers near her throat. The man was mad ... he was going to kill her. It couldn't be happening ... but it was. She was going to die here in a lonely barn, miles from home. The hands tightened around her neck. Blood pounded in her head. There was a roaring in her ears. Her last conscious thought as she slumped forward was that she had never seen so much hate in anyone's eyes as in his. ...

When Sharon came to, the nightmare had not ended. She suffered from a split second of total disorientation, when she did not know where she was. Then it all rushed back: the scuffle in the truck with Steve, the flight through the woods, the long walk in the rain, and the mad-eyed stranger in the barn. He was holding her now, carrying her through the darkness towards the house; he had put her sweater over her as a slight protection from the rain. Dazed and frightened, she began to struggle.

'Hold still,' he said repressively.

'Put me down—I don't want to go in the house with you!' To her horror she could hear the thin edge of hysteria in her voice.

'I'm not going to hurt you.'

He was taking her round the side of the house, unlatching a screen door and hooking it open with his foot, then pushing the other door open ahead of him. They were in a back porch, a row of hooks holding overalls and rainslickers, caps and sweaters, all neatly hung up. Unceremoniously he lowered her to the ground.

The room whirled and spun. Because it was the nearest thing, Sharon clutched at the front of his sweater, holding on tightly until the floor and the ceiling regained their proper relationship to each other. Then, and only then, did she look up at her rescuer.

He hates me holding on to him, she thought in a flash of intuition, her hand dropping to her side as if it had been stung. He hates me being here . . . but why? Trying to stop herself from shivering, she searched his face for clues.

His blond hair was thick and unruly, bleached to lightness by the sun. His eyes were blue, although that seemed too tame a word to describe their depth and brilliance. They were deep-set, a fan of tiny lines at the corners bespeaking a man who spent much time outdoors, as did the mahogany tan of his skin. The jutting cheekbones and the hard angle of his jaw were too full of strength and character for classic handsomeness; her overall impression was one of intense masculinity and, oddly enough, a deep and ever-present tiredness.

The silence had stretched on long enough. Sharon said bleakly, 'You don't want me here.'

'No, I don't. But you are here, and not even I can leave you out in the barn on a night like this when you're wet and cold. You'd better come in.'

She had never been made to feel so unwelcome anywhere in her life, not even at the hospital during the worst of her time there. If she had had her backpack, or even her poncho, she would have turned around and gone back out of the door regardless of the consequences. But as it was, she knew she had no choice but to stay.

There was a chair by the door. She sank down on it and bent over, fumbling with the laces of her boots, her fingers awkward with cold. Muttering something impatient under his breath, the man knelt at her feet and swiftly undid the laces, easing her feet out of the boots.

He had beautiful hair, she thought irrelevantly. The kind of hair a woman would want to run her fingers through ... realising that he was waiting for her to get up, she lowered her lashes in confusion and got to her feet. He led her through another door into the kitchen, where a single lamp over the sink cast a warm yellow glow over the room. It had all the modern conveniences; it was spotlessly clean, the polished pine cupboards and sand-coloured flooring obviously of excellent quality. Yet her general impression was one of starkness, of an almost clinical bareness. No curtains at the windows, no plants or bunches of herbs hanging from the hand-hewn beams in the ceiling. A man's room ... to her chagrin she heard her unruly tongue say, more statement than question, 'You're not married.'

'No, I'm not married.' His voice gave nothing away. 'If it's the proprieties you're worried about, although I'd have hardly thought that would have applied in your case, I do have a manservant who lives here. How long since you've eaten?'

'This morning,' she said defensively.

'I'll heat up some soup while you have a shower.'

'Please don't bother——'

'No trouble,' was the impersonal reply. 'Follow me.'

Again she was wise enough to know she had no choice; besides, the very thought of a hot shower was reviving in itself. Down the hallway from the kitchen the man pushed open the door into the bathroom. Spacious and immaculately clean, it had the same air of spartan masculinity as the kitchen. He said briefly, 'Wear that robe on the door. I'll put your clothes in the dryer while you're eating.' He backed out, pulling the door shut behind him.

Without even thinking, Sharon snapped the lock in place, for the first time in several hours feeling safe, at least temporarily. Opening a long cupboard, she helped herself from the stock of thick, fluffy white towels; there was soap and shampoo on the edge of the bath. About to pull her shirt over her head, she caught sight of

herself in the mirror, and with a twinge of humour
could almost find herself sympathising with the cold-
eyed stranger: she looked a wreck. There was a streak
of mud on her chin, while her wet hair was plastered to
her skull and her face was ashen pale, her eyes
shadowed with weariness. She looked like a waif, she
thought uncharitably. Or a stray kitten, skinny, half
drowned, and pathetic.

Pulling her braid forward over her shoulder, she
undid the narrow leather thong that bound it, and then
undressed, dropping her clothes in a heap on the floor.
Naked, she stepped into the shower, closing her eyes
under the spray of hot water, feeling it run over her
shoulders and breasts, deliciously hot, as good for her
morale as for her physical being. Afterwards, she found
a brush and blow-dryer under the sink and dried her
long, thick hair, her last act being to put on the robe
that the man had indicated. It was made of midnight-
blue silk and was far too big for her; she folded it
around her body as best she could, belting it tightly
around her waist. Checking to see that she had left the
bathroom as clean and tidy as she had found it, she
squared her shoulders and unlocked the door.

Because the house was so large, the sounds of the
wind and the rain were diminished to a distant murmur.
Otherwise, there was complete silence. For a moment
Sharon hesitated, her nerves tightening. Had he got
tired of waiting for her and gone to bed? Or was he
merely biding his time, ready to resume his attack on
her? Her bare feet soundless on the smooth hardwood
flooring, she padded towards the kitchen door, through
which a bar of yellow light splashed out into the hall.
Moving as quietly as she could, she entered the room.

From the saucepan on the stove wafted a delicious
odour. On the pine dropleaf table a place had been set
for one with cutlery and plain white china, as well as a
loaf of homemade bread, a pottery butter dish and a
wooden cheeseboard. The dog Wolf was sitting under
the table, unwinking brown eyes regarding her with
interest, his heavy tail swishing a greeting. His front legs
were as thick as a man's wrists, tufts of long white hair

growing between his pads—an adaptation to the ice and snow of his native land, she was later to learn. Warily keeping her stance by the door, Sharon let her eyes travel around the room, her heart fluttering against her ribs as she saw the man. He was lying stretched out on a couch under the window, his eyes closed, the sound of his breathing quiet and rhythmic; there could be no doubt that he was asleep. She stepped closer, seeing the slow rise and fall of his chest, noticing for the first time how unusually dark his lashes were compared with his hair, how there was more than a hint of sensuality in his mouth, relaxed in sleep. He did not look nearly as formidable asleep as awake, she thought ruefully; he merely looked like a man who for too long had been driving himself to the limits of his endurance and who could no more have stayed awake while he waited for her than he could have stopped breathing.

To her surprise she found herself unwilling to disturb him, not so much because she was frightened of him but rather because of some intuition that he desperately needed the rest. She tiptoed over to the stove and lifted the lid of the saucepan, inhaling the spicy aroma of what appeared to be a thick vegetable soup. A bowl and a spoon had been put on top of the stove and she began ladling the soup out, her mouth watering.

'Feeling better?'

She jumped, splashing some hot soup on her hand and stifling an exclamation of pain. Turning to face him, she stated the obvious. 'I thought you were asleep—you scared me!'

He was sitting on the edge of the couch running his fingers through his hair. His eyes flicked over her. 'Did I now?'

'I don't even know your name.'

'Ross Bowen. And you're Sharon Reid from Montreal.'

There was nothing definite in his words to disturb her; nevertheless, she found herself flushing. 'That's right, Mr Bowen,' she said sharply.

He stood up, stretching lazily. His legs in the faded blue jeans were long and muscular; he was deep-chested and broad-shouldered, his bare forearms tanned and corded with muscle. Every one of his movements had a certain grace to it, she admitted unwillingly to herself, the grace that comes from perfect co-ordination and from muscles toned up by constant use. Eyeing her sardonically, he drawled, 'Under the circumstances Mr Bowen seems a touch too formal. Ross will do.'

What was the matter with her? Sharon wondered crossly, feeling the colour creep into her cheeks again under his scrutiny. Although she was realistic enough to realise that men often found her attractive, she had never really analysed why; she was not a vain girl, for her mother's spectacular, exquisitely cared-for beauty had always cast her in the shade. So now she was unaware of just how beautiful she looked in the lamplight, the curves of her body only hinted at in the over-large robe, her slim legs bare from mid-thigh. Her brows were black wings over eyes of so deep a blue as to be purple; her hair. long and straight, brushed smooth to hang down her back, was that true iridescent black that occurs so rarely.

The gap in the conversation, if it could be called a conversation, had gone on too long for her peace of mind. She said evenly, 'Aren't you having anything to eat?'

He walked over to the stove and it took an actual effort of will for her not to shrink back as he reached across her for the kettle. He was so large ... and her scanty attire put her so hopelessly at a disadvantage. 'I'll have a cup of tea,' he said casually. Then, a bite to his voice, he added, 'Where'd you get that bruise?'

She followed his eyes downward to see just above her knee an ugly contusion on her skin. 'I suppose it must have happened in the truck.'

'While you were defending your virtue?' he said sarcastically.

'Yes, just that,' she snapped.

'That's your story and you're sticking to it, eh?'

'It happens to be true.' She glared at him, the food forgotten. 'It's fine for you to laugh! You're over six feet tall and you must weigh a couple of hundred pounds. I don't. So when some guy gets it in his head that he wants a bit of fun at my expense, it's no joke.'

'Then perhaps you shouldn't be wandering the back roads after dark by yourself,' he replied silkily.

Patches of angry colour highlighting her cheekbones she retorted, 'So now it's my fault! That's the classic male argument—that if a woman gets in trouble, she was asking for it.'

For once speaking without a hint of scepticism, he said slowly, 'You have a point, I suppose. Why don't we sit down while you tell me what actually happened.'

She filled the bowl with soup and carried it over to the table, cutting herself a piece of bread and buttering it, glad that he seemed to have declared at least a partial truce.

The soup tasted as good as it had smelled, and as soon as she started to eat she realised she was ravenously hungry. He waited patiently until she had satisfied the worst of her hunger, putting a mug of steaming hot tea by her plate. Trying to speak as concisely and objectively as she could, she related the encounter with Steve, describing him and his truck as accurately as possible, and finishing with her decision to sleep in the barn rather than wake up the inhabitants of the house. When she had finished, she buried her nose in the mug of tea, wondering edgily with what sarcastic rejoinder he would greet her story.

With the air of one withholding judgment, he said levelly, 'There's a Steve Dorion who lives ten or fifteen miles from here, and who has a truck like the one you described. I know his reputation's not good.' He pushed back his chair. 'Tomorrow I'll take a drive over there and see if he has your pack.'

'You mean you believe, me?'

He looked at her sombrely. 'I don't know, Sharon.' In what seemed to her like a complete non sequitur, he said, 'Why did you react so strongly when I mentioned that you might be involved with drugs?'

Her face grew pinched. Even here, miles from Montreal, the past was pursuing her, she thought dully. Would there never be any escaping it? 'I'm sure you're imagining that.'

His voice hardened. 'No, I wasn't, and you know that as well as I do. So you're lying, Sharon. And if you'll lie about one thing, you'll lie about another.' He stood up. 'I've got to get some sleep. Come on, I'll show you your room.'

For a brief while she had felt that he was on her side, giving her a fair hearing. But now he had retreated from her, and in a way she could hardly blame him: she had lied. However, there was nothing she could say or do to change matters, so obediently she followed him down the hall past the bathroom to what was presumably a guestroom. It posed no surprises, for already she had grown to expect the spartan cleanliness, the hint of a monk's cell. Ross Bowen preceded her into the room, switching on the bedside light and drawing the curtains. 'Extra blankets in the cupboard,' he said economically. 'Get up when you feel like it—I'll leave a note for Jock that you're here.'

Jock was presumably the manservant he had mentioned earlier. 'Thank you,' she said awkwardly. 'And thank you for letting me stay here.' Even if you don't want me, she added silently to herself.

He made an indeterminate noise and without bothering to say goodnight, left the room. She stared after him, feeling tears prick under her lids. The last five months had brought her more than her share of rejection, and this final one seemed one too many. Swallowing hard, she scrubbed her eyes and turned down the bed. The sheets were plain white, but immaculate, the blankets and bedspread a matching dark brown. No flowered sheets here, she thought muzzily, sliding into bed with the robe still wrapped around her, and pulling the covers up to her chin. She reached over to turn off the light, then let her head drop to the pillow. She fell asleep instantly, the deep, dreamless sleep of total exhaustion.

CHAPTER TWO

THE dark brown curtains blocked out the morning light, so when Sharon awoke the room was gloomy, shadows lurking in the corners. She peered at her watch, to find it was only six-thirty. Punching the pillow to make it more comfortable, she tried to settle back to sleep again, cross with herself for having woken so early; it came of being on the early shift at the hospital for so long, she knew. But today she had no need to get up early, and as it was the first time she had slept in a bed since she had left Montreal, she would be foolish not to take advantage of it.

All very fine, but after she had tossed and turned for ten minutes, she gave up any pretensions that she would fall asleep again. She got out of bed and opened the bedroom door; on the floor outside her room were her clothes in a neat little heap, laundered, dry, and folded. She got dressed quickly, made the bed, leaving the robe at the foot of it, and went to the bathroom. The house was very quiet, so it was no surprise to find the kitchen empty, although the aroma of freshly ground coffee in the air told her someone had been there recently. Ross? Or the as yet unknown Jock?

Sunlight was pouring through the kitchen windows. Without stopping for thought Sharon crossed the room quickly and went out the back door, standing on the step and lifting her face to the sun's warmth. The kitchen faced an orchard where the rows of trees were newly leafed, the sky above them rinsed to a clear, pale blue by the rain. Raindrops sparkled in the grass, refracting the light into all the colours of the spectrum; even the ordinary dandelions this morning looked like gold medallions thrown in careless largesse among the trees.

Sharon drew a deep breath of the morning air: damp grass, the farmyard odour of manure, far from unpleasant, and nearer the heavy scent of the purple lilac blossoms in the garden, a perfect distillation of a summer morning. To her ears drifted the bawling of a calf, the mutter of machinery from one of the barns, the slam of a truck door and an exchange of male voices ending in laughter. Gazing up the hill between the apple trees, she knew she would like to walk up there and lie in the sun; she would like to pick an armful of the fragrant lilac and use it to soften the austerity of the house; she would like to be free to explore all the sights and sounds of the farm. It was all so beautiful yet equally so very real, that somehow she sensed she could feel at home here in a way she never had in the elegant artificiality of the house in Montreal.

Shocked by her own thoughts and knowing that to stay was a dream impossible of realisation, so unwelcoming had Ross Bowen been, she began to walk across the grass towards the barns. In the daylight she could see that the farm stood on a gradual slope, with above her the orchard and the road, then the barns, and then beyond them and below her a vast stretch of meadowland, patched like a quilt in squares of different colours: pale green, dark green, mud brown. Far in the distance was a long promontory, its steep cliffs the same brick-red; around its base she caught the illusory gleam of the sea. Again she was swept by the strange presentiment that she belonged here, that to leave would be denying some kind of basic need buried deep in her psyche. . . .

Giving herself a little shake, she walked briskly towards the barn where she had taken shelter the night before. The inside was dimly lit, dust motes drifting in the still air; from below came an intrusive metallic clattering and the high-pitched hum of a motor. She went partway down the stairs, ducking her head to avoid the low beams.

As she had already suspected, it was the dairy barn. Thirty or forty cattle stood in the metal stanchions, while about two-thirds the way down the row Ross Bowen was pouring a stream of milk from one metal container into another larger one. Then he disappeared from sight between two cows. For perhaps fifteen minutes she sat quietly watching him as he went from cow to cow with the automatic milkers. His progress seemed slow to her: it would have gone much quicker with two people, she thought critically. When she was sure he would not see her, she got up and went back outside.

This time when she went into the kitchen there was a man standing at the stove. She smiled uncertainly. 'Hello. I'm Sharon Reid—did Mr Bowen tell you about me?'

'Aye, he did. Jock MacKenzie's the name. Are you hungry?'

'Yes, I am. But I can——'

'Sit down, then, and I'll fix you up a bite.'

It was a tone of voice used to giving orders; as she did what she was told, Sharon couldn't help wondering with amusement if he ordered Ross around as well, and with what success. Not much, she'd be willing to bet. Jock was not much taller than she, his grizzled hair and beard neatly trimmed. He was wearing a white singlet under a spotless white apron, his bare arms so mottled with tattoes that serpents, sea monsters, and beautiful damsels were forced to co-exist in uneasy intimacy, brought to writhing life every time he moved his arms. Trying not to stare at them, and honest enough with herself to admit that she was searching for information, she said, 'It was very kind of Mr Bowen to let me stay.'

A sound that could have been either assent or dissent came from Jock as he expertly cracked two brown-shelled eggs over the frying pan.

She tried again. 'I was just down in the dairy barn watching him milk the cows. He must work very hard.'

'He does that. Too hard. He'll break his heart over this place yet.' He wielded the bread knife fiercely. 'One or two pieces of toast, miss?'

'Two, if I may.' Why would Ross Bowen be breaking his heart over a farm? 'He must have help, though?'

'Indeed, yes—but it's hard to get good people. The fellow who was helping him milk upped and left two days ago. His girl-friend wasn't seeing enough of him, he said.' Jock's voice was laced with scorn as he expertly flipped the eggs.

A crazy idea shot through Sharon's brain, leaving her weak with longing. 'You mean he has to do all the milking by himself now?' she said carefully. A nod of acknowledgment as Jock buttered the toast. 'Couldn't one of the other men help him?'

'They're not trained, for one thing. And they're needed for the haying—the first crop's about ready. Early this year.' He put a plate of bacon and eggs in front of her, then brought a mug of coffee and toast. 'Eat up, lass. You're thin enough that the crows could carry you off.'

'I won't be if I eat all that,' she retorted pertly, watching a reluctant grin tug at his mouth.

He passed her a jar of jam, one of the serpents leering at her horribly. 'This is the day I go to town for supplies, so if you'll excuse me, miss, I'll be on my way. Make yourself at home, won't you?'

If only she could.... 'Has he advertised yet for someone to replace the man who left?' she blurted.

'Hasn't got around to it, I don't think.' Jock shot her a shrewd glance as he took off his apron, hanging it on a hook by the door. 'He's not an easy man to work for, drives everyone else as hard as he drives himself.'

'I see.' Sharon bent her head, fiddling with her toast. 'Well, thank you for breakfast.'

'Pleasure, miss.'

Sharon finished eating, washed and dried the dishes and put them away in the cupboards, unsurprised to find the china and glasses arranged on the shelves with mathematical precision. On the top shelf she saw a tall cut glass vase. Standing on a chair, she got it down, took a knife from the drawer, and went outside. It was no trouble to cut half a dozen branches from the blossom-laden bushes; carrying them back inside, she arranged them in the vase and put it in the middle of the kitchen table, then stood back to admire her handiwork. It was remarkable how one vase of flowers could change the look of a room, she decided, half appalled at her own temerity, yet knowing she had needed in some small way to imprint her own personality here. Once she was gone, she would at least be remembered for as long as the flowers lasted. And, of course, she would have to leave. . . . Restlessly she went outside again. Below the house was a fair-sized vegetable garden, the seedlings in such straight rows that she was sure it was part of Jock's domain. But there were also several flower beds, including a rose garden and a perennial border, all in a state of bad neglect. Even the lawn could have done with mowing. By poking around in the toolshed she found a trowel, a hoe, and a bucket, and soon she was on her knees pulling out the weeds and loosening the earth around the perennials, enjoying the sun on her back and the chatter of birdsong from the orchard. It was all so peaceful, and so far away from the place she had called home: she wished it could go on for ever.

A couple of hours must have passed before subconsciously she heard the car draw up by the house. But she did not connect it in any way with herself. She was wrestling with a clump of crab grass that had entangled itself with the delphiniums when a voice spoke behind her. 'Did you put the flowers in the kitchen?'

She shook the earth from the mass of roots, dumped the grass in the bucket, and only then got to her feet, slowly turning to face Ross Bowen. With the sun bleaching his hair to fairness and his eyes reiterating the blue of the sky behind him, he was even more devastatingly attractive than she remembered. The dog Wolf was sitting at his heels. 'Good morning,' she said, as casually as she could. 'Yes, I did.'

'The woman's touch.'

Although his expression was unreadable, Sharon found herself blushing. 'I thought they looked nice.'

'So they do. I got your pack, by the way.'

'Oh . . . thank you.'

'Once Jock gets back from town, I'll get him to drive you as far as the main road so you can get on your way again.'

'I see.' She brushed the worst of the mud from her

hands to give herself time to collect her thoughts. 'Did you have any trouble getting my things?'

'No,' Ross said grimly. 'Steve was in a tight spot and he knew it. It'll be a while before he tries anything like that again.' With reluctant admiration he added, 'He's got a mean set of scratch marks on his face.'

She laughed outright. 'Good!' she said with great satisfaction.

It was the first time he had seen her laugh. His eyes trained on her face, he said, 'So that much of your story was true, at least.'

It was now or never. . . . Her nails digging into her palms, she said, 'Jock tells me you're shorthanded in the dairy barn. I've no experience on a farm, but I learn fast and I'm not afraid of hard work.'

There was a charged silence and she had the fleeting impression that she had taken him completely by surprise. 'You're offering yourself for the job?' he said in a neutral voice.

'That's right.' Her words came out louder than she had expected and she swallowed nervously.

'My dear girl, do you have any idea what's involved? Cows need milking twice a day, seven days a week. You're up at four-thirty in the morning and you often don't get to bed until ten. You'd be expected to help out with the heifers, and the haying, and with anything else that happens to come along—and on a farm there's always something. The pay's not great and it's hard, heavy work.' He looked her up and down disparagingly. 'Man's work.'

Sharon flushed angrily. 'The last person you had was a man, and that didn't work out. Besides, I'm stronger than I look.'

'How old are you?'

It was an unexpected question. 'Twenty-three.'

'So you're not a kid just out of high school. What was your last job—and why did you leave?'

She licked her lips. 'Is that relevant?'

'I would have thought so.' As she remained silent, he added, 'So you're not going to tell me. Can you give me references?'

'No.'

The monosyllable hung in the air between them. 'Were you in trouble with the law?'

She said carefully, 'I don't have a criminal record, if that's what you mean.'

'That's not quite what I asked, is it?' His face hardened. 'As far as the job's concerned, the answer's no.'

From the direction his questions had taken she had known he was going to refuse her; nevertheless, it was a crushing disappointment. She turned her face away, not wanting him to see what a blow it had been.

In quite a different tone of voice Ross asked, 'Why do you want this job so much?'

Again he had taken her by surprise. Tricked into honesty, she said in a low voice, 'I don't know if I can even explain that to myself. It's something about the place—so beautiful, yet so rooted in reality.' She shrugged helplessly. 'That doesn't sound like much of a reason, does it? But it's the best I can do.'

'Where were you heading originally?'

'Towards Riverford. I have a—a relative there. I was planning to visit her.'

'Won't she be expecting you?'

She lowered the thick fringe of her lashes. 'No,' she said very quietly. 'She's not expecting me.'

'Look at me.' Her eyes flew upward. 'You're a strange mixture, Sharon Reid. You turn up out of nowhere with a story that's as full of holes as a sieve. I know you've been less than truthful to me. But——' He raked his fingers through his hair, his expression full of exasperation. 'I don't even know why I'm doing this. I'll probably regret it. You can start this evening. I'll give you a week's trial. You can stay in the same room you slept in last night and Jock will provide all your meals. You'll get minimum wage. Any questions?'

'No,' she murmured breathlessly. Her smile broke out, radiating her face, brightening her eyes to the shade of spring violets. 'Thank you!'

'Yeah . . . well, that's that.' He ran his fingers around the collar of his shirt and she sensed he was already regretting his reversed decision. 'I've got to get to work—be in the barn at four.' He disappeared into the house, Wolf padding after him, leaving her standing alone in the sunlight.

The first days at Marshwinds Farm passed in a whirl of activity for Sharon, for there was so much to learn and so little time to do it in. She learned how to put on the milkers and, more difficult, when to take them off; she learned the personal idiosyncrasies of all the cows, a mixed herd of purebred Guernseys and Holsteins; she learned how to clean all the equipment, how to feed the heifers, how to bring the cows up from the meadow. And everything she learned seemed to lead to a dozen new questions.

As a trained nurse she was no stranger to machinery, and besides, she was quick and intelligent and more than willing to learn. Ross Bowen treated her as impersonally as if she were a boy, never touching her, never addressing any remarks of a personal nature to her, but his explanations were always complete and easily comprehensible, and she grew to respect his breadth of knowledge and his dedication to the rolling acres that were his home. Yet she was no nearer to knowing him. If there was no repetition of his corrosive anger towards her that first night in the barn, there was equally no warmth. She was simply one of the farmhands, who might or might not work out; as a person, certainly as a woman, she failed to exist for him. Because she was so busy, her brain so overloaded with new information all of which had to be remembered and put to use, she had little time to repine over his attitude; her sole ambition was for the quality of her work to satisfy his high standards.

Five days after she had arrived at the farm, they were just starting the evening milking when one of the farmhands came into the barn with the news that the tractor in the hundred-acre field had broken down. Ross hesitated only briefly. 'You carry on, Sharon,' he said. 'I'll be back in an hour.'

She merely nodded, but she knew with an inner glow

of satisfaction that she must have proved herself to him or he would never have left her. Strapping the milking stool around her waist, she got to work, taking her time and remembering all her instructions. She had milked eight cows and was leaning her forehead against the silky flank of one of the Guernseys while she attached the milker when a man's voice spoke above the hum of the suction pump. 'Ross? You in here?'

Finishing what she was doing, she stepped out into the cement aisle. 'Ross isn't here,' she started to say.

The man who was walking towards her at first glance was a replica of Ross Bowen. But when he halted a couple of feet away from her, she saw that her first impression was erroneous. The hair was coarser and darker, the eyes hazel and curiously pale, while the flesh on the heavily boned face was already sagging, pouches beneath the eyes. He was slightly shorter than Ross, with the thick waistline of a man who spent too much time at a desk. Yet despite all these differences, there was still an uncanny sense of resemblance. As the pale eyes ran over her from head to foot, she shifted uncomfortably, not sure what she disliked about him, only knowing she did.

'So you're the new farmhand,' he said, with a familiarity she instantly resented. 'I must say you're an improvement on the last one.' His eyes dropped to the jut of her breasts under her overalls. 'Quite an improvement.'

She said coldly, 'Were you looking for Mr Bowen?'

'For Ross, yes. I'm his older brother, Greg Bowen.'

He held out his hand. Sharon smiled insincerely, having no desire to touch him. 'I'd better not shake hands, Mr Bowen, I'm not very clean. Ross went to fix a tractor, he should be back any minute.' She looked pointedly at his polished leather Oxfords. 'If you want to wait up at the house, I'll tell Ross you're here.'

'No, no, I'll wait here.' He leaned against one of the posts. 'Jock told me Ross had a new helper, but not how pretty she was. And you're living in the house, eh? Good for Ross!'

Scarlet colour flooded her cheeks. 'Mr Bowen, if

you're insinuating that Ross and I are involved in any way other than on an employer-employee basis, you couldn't be more wrong. Now, if you'll excuse me, I have work to do.'

He put a hand on her wrist. 'Don't be in such a hurry.'

He was standing far too close for comfort; she could smell the cloying odour of his after-shave. She shook his hand off, repeating coldly, 'I think it would be much better if you waited up at the house.'

Incautiously she turned her back on him, bending over to pick up a milk can. Without finesse he grabbed her from behind, his hands fumbling for her breasts. For a moment she was rigid with shock, then she twisted in his hold, her eyes blazing with rage. 'Take your hands off me!' she hissed, jabbing at him with her elbows.

He was stronger than he looked. One arm clamped itself around her waist, pushing her back against the post, the other hand forced her chin up. His mouth landed full on hers, the wet thrust of his lips a violation. Unable to move, unable to breathe, she felt her head begin to spin.

'Let go of her, Greg.'

Sharon's mouth was freed, and she drew a long, ragged breath. Greg said jocularly, 'Well, you know me, little brother. When it's offered, I'm not about to turn it down——'

Almost choking with rage, Sharon cried, 'You know darn well I didn't——'

Ross's voice cut across hers. 'Shut up, Sharon—don't make it worse than it is by lying.'

'I'm not!'

His mouth twisted with scorn, Ross added, 'You and my brother are two of a kind—you'd make a good pair. But I'm paying you to work, not to tumble in the hay with Greg——'

'Really, Ross,' Greg interrupted smoothly, 'aren't you being a bit hard on the girl? It was only a little kiss, after all.'

Ross said dispassionately, 'You haven't taken over

the place yet, Greg—so don't try and tell me how to treat my employees.'

'Ah, yes ... which brings me to the reason for my visit,' Greg responded smoothly. 'Perhaps we should go somewhere more private?'

Bewildered by undercurrents about which she knew nothing, Sharon saw Ross's face tighten as his hands clenched at his sides, as if he was bracing himself for something unpleasant. He owned Marshwinds, didn't he, she thought uncertainly. So how could Greg take it over? What threat did he represent?

'I have to finish up here first,' Ross rejoined coolly. 'Go on up to the house. Jock will make you a drink. Just don't ask him to join you, okay, Greg?'

Greg raised a plump hand in mocking salute. 'I never pull the same trick twice, now do I, Ross? Delighted to have met you, Sharon—no doubt our paths will cross again.'

Not if I can help it, the girl thought, barely acknowledging his departure. She turned to face Ross. 'I didn't——'

'Leave it, Sharon,' he said wearily, his blue eyes bleak. 'Let's get on with this.'

She turned away, frustrated by his refusal to listen to her. Dipping the nozzles into the disinfectant solution and wiping them with paper towels, she decided to try another tack. 'Why can't Jock have a drink?'

His back to her, Ross said flatly, 'Because he's an alcoholic. One drop of the stuff and he's gone. A leftover from his Navy days, I'm afraid. About six months ago Greg thought it would be fun to slip him a drink of rum—it took me two weeks to sober Jock up.'

'You mean Greg knew beforehand what would happen?' she gasped, horrified.

'Oh, yes. When he was a kid he used to pull the wings off butterflies.'

She pounced. 'Yet you immediately assumed *I* was the one who started that kiss!'

'Well, you do have to admit it's a bit coincidental—

first Steve, now Greg, and all within five days. Are you always more sinned against than sinning, Sharon?'

The milking forgotten, she said levelly, 'Do you despise all women, or is it only me?'

'Don't push me, Sharon.'

Recklessly she ignored his warning. 'You mean you can say whatever you like about me, but I'm not allowed to reply in kind? What sort of a double standard is that, Ross?' Getting angrier by the minute, she swept on, 'Just who the *hell* do you think you are, that you're immune to criticism?'

'It's not who the hell I am—it's who the hell you are, Sharon Reid.' He had forgotten about the milking. He took a step closer to her; she could see the corded muscles in his neck and the tension in the set of his shoulders and fought back the urge to retreat. 'You're running away from something, aren't you?'

'So what if I am? That's not considered a criminal offence!'

His voice was dangerously quiet. 'Not even when it's to do with drugs?'

She could not have prevented her tell-tale recoil if she had tried. Her mouth dry, she said flatly, 'Ross, I swear to you I have never taken drugs in my life.'

Neither of them noticed he was now gripping her by the shoulders. 'So what were you doing—supplying them to someone else?' he demanded roughly 'In my books that's a thousand times worse.'

It was exactly what she had been accused of. As if it was yesterday, she was back in the boardroom at the hospital facing the array of cold, impersonal faces around the oval table and the horrifying build-up of evidence against her, and all the disbelief and humiliation and fear came washing over her again, drowning her in a nightmare world where sanity and reason had vanished.

He was shaking her, his voice a vicious thread. 'So that was it—I can tell by looking at you. Have you no idea of the suffering you were responsible for? Or didn't you even care?'

Numbly she saw the same inhuman fury flare in his

face as she had seen that windy, rain-swept night she had arrived here. Limp as a rag doll, she suffered his hold, knowing with the bitterness of defeat that he would never believe her, even if she did tell him the truth. Roger, who had professed to love her, had not believed her. So why should Ross believe her when he had made no secret of his contempt for her?

Perhaps it was her silence that further enraged him. He said through gritted teeth, 'You're the most beautiful woman I've ever seen in my life, and you've got the morals of a tramp, haven't you? A cheap little tramp.' He grinned wolfishly. 'I'm beginning to wonder what Steve and Greg have got that I haven't. Why don't we find out?'

A split second before he reached out for her she realised his intention, and her whole body stiffened. It had been bad enough to be kissed by Steve and by Greg, but somehow she knew it would be infinitely worse to be kissed by Ross Bowen. Steve and Greg she could in some way dismiss, but not Ross. . . . She pushed against his chest with the palms of her hands, her eyes wide with panic. 'Don't!' she gasped. 'Please, Ross——'

The arms that went around her had ten times her strength. He drew her inexorably closer until the whole length of her body was pressed against his own. Only then did he raise her chin with fingers like a steel vice and lower his head until his lips seized hers. She struggled against him, twisting and writhing, but it was a futile expenditure of energy; she was as helpless as an animal caught in a trap. She allowed her body to go limp, hoping he would relax his stranglehold on her, but if anything his grip tightened. Briefly she ceased struggling, knowing it was useless, and as she did so became aware of other sensations.

It was a kiss he had begun in anger, she knew. Yet as she held herself very still under his assault, scarcely breathing, hating the unforgiving demands of his mouth just as she had hated Steve's and Greg's, she felt the change in him. A strange hesitation, as if he had opened a door and found himself in a room different from the one he had expected. A gentling of his kiss. The hand that had been clamped against her waist began very slowly to run up and down her back, insinuating itself under her overalls to massage the long indentation of her spine. She felt his other hand lift the heavy weight of her hair, his fingers seeking the soft hollows at the nape of her neck. His lips were warm and very sure of themselves.

She could not have said when her resistance changed to passivity and passivity to pleasure. She only knew that tentatively she began to return the probing of his kiss, that her lips parted and that she welcomed the first, dizzying exploration of her mouth. Her body grew pliant in his arms; her hands reached up to cup his face, her fingers burying themselves in the thick, unexpectedly silky hair; her blood was racing through her veins. Even through the layers of clothing that separated them, she could feel the heavy pounding of his heart and with a thrill of primitive pride she knew he was as affected as she.

She also knew she had never been kissed like this before. Kissing Roger had been pleasant enough, but there had never been any danger of her losing control of the situation; with a stab of certainty she knew that if Ross chose to carry this embrace further, she would be unable to resist him: would, in fact, welcome it. A delicious weakness spread through her limbs as for the first time in her life she gained an inkling of the explosive forces that could be generated between man and woman.

When he thrust her away the shock was all the greater for this new-found knowledge, and his words, harsh and ugly, were an instant repudiation of that fragile sense of wonder. He snarled, 'You like them all, don't you, Sharon? Steve. Greg. Me. It's all the same to you. The token struggle and then the come-on.' He rubbed the back of his hand against his mouth as if trying to erase the touch of her lips. 'There's a word for women like you!'

'You're wrong,' she stammered, too shocked to be anything but honest. 'Ross, it's not like that——'

'Spare me the wide-eyed innocence, okay?' he said heavily. 'And let's get something straight right now—if you're going to fool around with Greg, you won't do it here at Marshwinds. Do you understand?'

Against her back she could feel the roughness of the post, comfortingly solid; she seemed to draw strength from it. 'I understand completely,' she said coldly. 'You're determined to think the worst of me, no matter what the situation, that's what I understand. Go ahead, Ross Bowen—I can't stop you.' Pointedly she picked up the nearest milk can, hoping he hadn't noticed that her hand was trembling. 'And now we'd better get to work, hadn't we?'

He muttered an oath under his breath, turning his back on her, and in total silence they began working their way along the two parallel rows of animals. Sharon, on her part, was trying not to think at all about that single devastating kiss and all it purported, forcing herself instead to concentrate on the safe, routine actions as she went from cow to cow, taking comfort from their warmth and stolidity.

Noticing that Ross was going to finish a bit ahead of her, she said with frigid politeness, 'I'll clean everything up if you want to go and talk to your brother.'

'Thank you,' was the equally chilly response. 'But I'd better wait and check the valves on the milk tank.'

She knew he was right to do so, for if she didn't adjust them correctly, hundreds of gallons of milk would go down the drain. He came over to her side to help her finish, then while she carried the equipment into the pump room where the big stainless steel sinks were, he rolled up the plastic hose that pumped the milk into the tank, draining the valves and washing out the hose. 'That's it,' he said finally. 'Can you finish up?'

'Yes.'

'Sharon, I—oh, hell, what's the use? I'll be up at the house if you need me.'

He strode out of the door, letting it bang shut behind him. The pump room was very warm, and wearily Sharon leaned against the counter, wiping her forehead on her sleeve as for the first time she began to question the wisdom of her decision to stay at Marshwinds. To work for a man who despised her was bad enough. But when the same man had the power to arouse sensations in her that she had not even known existed, that was ten times worse. Maybe the wisest thing she could do would be to hand in her notice—and thereby confirm his bad opinion of her, she thought wryly. Oh, well...

She filled the sink with water, adding the correct amounts of disinfectant. Then she went back into the barn to get the last two milk cans, which were down at the far end under the hayloft; as she bent to pick them up, she heard from overhead the sound of Ross's voice, as clear as if he were in the same room. 'I thought you were going to wait in the house.'

Her hesitation was fatal. She had no wish to eavesdrop, but neither did she want the clatter of the milkers to give away her presence. She stood very still, knowing that Greg's would be the voice she would hear in response.

'Jock makes it so painfully clear that he loathes the ground I walk on that I didn't particularly want to wait up there. You do inspire such touching loyalty, little brother.'

Although she could not see him, Sharon could pick up the tension underlying Ross's words. 'You didn't come all the way out here to discuss Jock. Get to the point, Greg.'

'Yes ... well.' A pause, as though Greg was enjoying keeping his brother in suspense. 'As you know, my option to sell Marshwinds runs out at the end of the summer. I've decided to exercise it, Ross.'

The pause was longer this time. 'I see. I thought you probably would. When, Greg, and for how much?'

'You disappoint me, Ross,' Greg replied softly. 'I'd expected more of a reaction than that.'

'Hoped for more of a reaction, you mean. You're still pulling the wings off the butterflies, aren't you, Greg?'

'I'm doing nothing that I'm not legally entitled to do.'

'Quite true. What you're doing is also despicable—but you don't need me to tell you that, do you?'

'It's purely a business matter.'

'Don't kid yourself—you've hated my guts ever since I was born. How fortunate for you that our late, lamented father was obliging enough to present you with the opportunity to nail me to the wall. Which I gather you are about to do.'

Sharon felt a chill go down her spine at the open hostility in Greg's voice. 'You're right, Ross—let's quit kidding ourselves. It's going to give me a great deal of pleasure to nail you. I've waited a long time, haven't I?'

'Five years—long enough. But you didn't answer my question, Greg—when and how much?'

'The end of August. Three-quarters of a million.'

There was a silence that went on for too long. 'You know damn well I haven't got a hope in hell of raising that amount.'

'Exactly.'

'You're a bastard, Greg.'

Sharon could almost see the expression of gloating on Greg's features. 'Wrong again, Ross. You're the bastard, remember?'

'You've never forgiven her for that, have you?'

'No. And as she's been dead for years, it's an academic question anyhow. But to get back to the other matter—I think I'm being more than fair. You've got over two months to come up with the money. After all, I could have waited to tell you until the end of August, couldn't I?'

'If you're expecting thanks, you'll wait a long time.' Another pause, as Sharon waited with bated breath. 'Look, Greg, I won't get down on my knees for you or anyone else. But you know as well as I do that you don't want Marshwinds—you've never been remotely interested in the place. Your life is in the city.' Ross's voice deepened with emotion. 'But I love the place, Greg. I've worked here for years. I've walked over every inch of it. The orchards, the fields, the streams—I know them all, and I love them, winter and summer, day and night. The place is in my bones ... offer it to me at a decent price, Greg, one I can afford. Because you don't need the money, we both know that, don't we?'

Another of those difficult pauses. 'Let me stay here, where I belong.'

'Well, well, who would have thought it?' Greg said smoothly. 'Ross Bowen begging for mercy! Very touching, Ross, very touching indeed. However, much as I hate to disappoint you, the date and the price stand. I'm sure you can find an understanding banker somewhere who'll help you out.'

'With interest rates the way they are? You know damn well I can't!'

'Perhaps you're right . . . pity. Well, if you can't buy Marshwinds, I'm sure I'll find someone who can. It's what they call in the real estate business a very desirable property.'

'I've had enough of this, Greg. Get in your car and go back to the city. You can send me a formal notice of your price and the date—not that I don't trust you, you understand.'

'It will be a pleasure. . . . So long, Ross. Don't work too hard!'

Sharon heard the fall of footsteps across the floor and then, a couple of minutes later, the sound of a car engine starting up . . . so Greg was gone. From above her head there was only silence. Then she jumped as there came a loud thump, as if something had been flung against the wall. Another thud of footsteps, these heavier, angrier. The slam of the barn door and then silence again.

CHAPTER THREE

VERY slowly Sharon picked up the milk cans and walked back into the pump room, her head whirling with the implications of what she had overheard. Ross did not own Marshwinds: that much was clear. Greg did. How or why she was not sure, although apparently their dead father had been at the root of it. And now Greg was going to sell Marshwinds, at a price Ross could not afford. Which menat Ross would have to leave the place he so dearly loved. . . .

Why should that matter to her? she thought, scrubbing the rubber nozzles with the brush and rinsing them off. It wasn't as if Ross had made any efforts to gain her sympathy or liking: he had treated her with anger, coldness, and scorn. So why did she now find her heart aching for him as she went back over that conversation between the two brothers, remembering with painful clarity how Ross, proud, independent Ross, had humbled himself in front of Greg, pleading for a fair price . . . how deeply he must want to keep Marshwinds in order to do that!

She finished up the chores and went up to the house, where she ate a late supper by herself in the kitchen; there was no sign of Jock or Ross. Then she went to her room and read for a while, but she could not concentrate on the words on the page. Restlessly she wandered over to the window and gazed out. Beyond the heifer barn she could see the gateway that led down to the meadows; Ross was steering a tractor through the opening, while one of the farmhands closed the gate behind him. He had probably been mowing in one of the alfalfa fields, she decided idly, remembering how pleased he had been at the possibility of getting three crops this summer rather than the usual two. If Greg sold the farm, whether there were two crops or three would become immaterial, she thought, watching Ross jump to the ground, exchange a few words with the other man, and then stride up towards the house. As he got closer, she moved back a little, not wanting him to see her. He was staring down at the ground, his hands thrust deep in his pockets, vertical frown lines scoring his forehead. When he came level with the house, he hesitated for a moment before walking past it to go up the hill.

Sharon stood irresolutely. Mind your own business, her brain argued, coldly and rationally. Ross Bowen is nothing to you. So what if he's going to lose his farm? It's no concern of yours. . . . Yes, it is, the warm, feminine part of her nature argued back. Maybe just having someone to talk to would help. . . . Oh sure, her brain retorted cynically. What you mean is, you're hoping he'll kiss you again. . . . I'm not! I only want to help. . . .

Without consciously having made a decision, she went outside. Ross was no longer in sight, but if she went up the hill she was fairly sure she would meet him. She walked between the parallel rows of apple trees where the fruit was beginning to emerge from the bud, small and hard and green. The grass had been mowed only a few days ago, and all the sweet scents of summer seemed to be hanging between the green-leafed boughs under a slowly darkening sky. High in the heavens the first star shone fitfully.

She had reached the crest of the hill. Passing between the trees, she came to the boundary of the orchard, where an electric fence separated it from one of the pastures. Ross was leaning on the gate, his back to her.

For a moment she stood still. In the west the sun was close to the horizon, a vivid orange sphere in a glowing sky that was fading from orange to pale gold, with the scattered clouds like dark bars across it. The faraway cape seemed to be suspended in a gilded sea. A tractor was driving away from them across the vast expanse of dykeland; otherwise there was no sound, no movement, only the somnolent peace of a summer evening.

How could he bear to give it up? Sharon thought in anguish. The acres spread in front of him were his in a way they could never be Greg's. So beautiful, so well loved. She took a hesitant step forward. With a chirp of alarm a robin took to the air, startling her and causing Ross's head to swing around. Across the forty feet or so that separated them, he demanded, 'What do you want? Is something wrong?'

'No . . . I just felt like a walk. It's such a beautiful evening,' she said banally, crossing the grass towards him.

As if he was noticing the glorious sunset for the first time, he said flatly, 'It is, I suppose. Sharon, I hate to sound rude, but I came up here to be alone.'

'Why, Ross?' she asked very quietly.

His back was to the sun so that his facial expression was hidden from her. 'It's no concern of yours.'

She ventured, 'You're worried about something.'

'Sharon, leave it, will you?' His voice was rough with impatience.

How foolish she'd been to think he might need her help ... she turned away, her shoulders slumped, muttering, 'I'm sorry if I intruded,' and began to walk back the way she'd come.

'Sharon——' She turned her head. His features an inscrutable mask, he said, 'Do you feel like going for a walk? Or are you too tired?'

It was an olive branch, and one she was only too happy to accept. 'No, I'm not too tired—I'd like that. Could we go down on the dykes? I've never been down there.'

'Sure. We can go through the pasture.'

Sharon had discovered in the few days she had been at Marshwinds that the acres of meadowland below the farm were known locally as the dykes, the reason being that the Bay of Fundy tides, the highest in the world, were held back all along the perimeter of the fields by an abutment of earth and stone, miles long. The dykes proper had first been built nearly three hundred years ago by the Acadians, transplanted Frenchmen who had settled the area and tilled the rich soil until they were deported by the British in the mid-seventeen-hundreds; to this day it was said that no one could manage the system of dykes as well as the Acadians had with their primitive tools so many years ago. So for Sharon the area was haunted with the ghosts of the men, women, and children who had called this place home, and then, for political expediency, had been uprooted and carried away in tall ships to the seaboard of the American colonies, or back to France.

As if he had read her thoughts, Ross said softly, 'At dusk, like this, one can almost put the clock back, can't one? Do you see that gully over there? Supposedly that's where they loaded the Acadians on to boats to row them out to the ships anchored in the basin. Family members were separated, they say, never to see each other again. And their houses and barns were burned to the ground behind them. . . .' He laughed shortly, a sound without humour. 'Maybe the place is cursed.'

She thought she had her opening. 'Why do you say that?'

'Because—oh, never mind.'

So he would not share his troubles with her. . . . They were tramping along the edge of a hayfield where the grass grew tall and luxuriant; the last tiny arc of the sun had slipped beneath the horizon. Ross was striding along like a man possessed, his shoulders hunched, his eyes to the ground, but wisely Sharon made no complaint, knowing that physical activity was probably the best thing for him. They must have walked for well over half an hour, by which time they were near the eastern line of the dykes. Water filled the gullies, which widened out into a reedy pond; as Sharon and Ross approached, a pair of black ducks exploded into the air and wheeled towards the west, their long-necked bodies and fast-beating wings black silhouettes against the fading light.

Sharon watched them until they were out of sight, something wistful in her upturned face; she was quite unaware that Ross was watching her, rather than the ducks. 'Weren't they beautiful?' she murmured, more to herself than to him.

'Beautiful,' he agreed, an odd note in his voice making her glance up quickly. She could feel the colour creep into her face, for she was achingly aware of the strange attraction this man had for her, and somehow frightened by it. She said abruptly, 'Can we walk up on the dyke?'

His face hardened fractionally. 'Of course.'

She followed him across a culvert and along a narrow dirt track that brought them to the base of the dyke. They clambered up the grassy slope to the top, where there was a well-beaten track wide enough for a tractor; the seaward slope was reinforced with rocks, the whole structure much larger than she had expected. Seeing her interest, Ross commented, 'You can go for miles along the dykes following the courses of all the tidal rivers as well as the shoreline.'

She saw now that they were standing near the estuary of a river. The tide was out, exposing the riverbed, a deep channel in the smooth and glutinous red mud, surrounded by acres of tidal flats covered with tough, pliable marsh grass. A full moon was hanging low over the horizon casting a ghostly light over everything, so that the mud flats took on the dull sheen of pewter and the stream in the riverbed became a winding silver ribbon. From the pond behind them came the muted peeping of frogs; otherwise they were enshrouded in silence.

By a kind of unspoken agreement they sat down on a grassy spot on the bank, Sharon content to drink in the eerie beauty of the scene. The moment stretched into minutes, until some sixth sense told her she was being watched. She looked over at her companion. He was staring at her fixedly, such a strained intensity in his expression that her heart skipped a beat. 'What's wrong, Ross?' she asked softly, the sound of her voice almost an intrusion in the quiet night.

The words seemed to be forced out of him. 'I'm going to lose Marshwinds, Sharon.'

She sat up a little straighter, despite her concern for him aware of an unbidden thrill of pleasure that he had, after all, chosen to confide in her. 'How can that happen?'

'I don't own it—my brother Greg does.'

'But I thought you did.'

'So do most people. I've lived here for ten years now, ever since I got out of agricultural school; I built it up from virtually nothing to what it is today. But it's never been mine.'

With the intuition that she might be stepping on dangerous ground, she asked bluntly, 'Why not?'

He was shredding a long blade of grass into thin strips. 'It's a long story, and an unhappy one. I've never told anyone about it before, Sharon. . . .'

In the moonlight his eyes had darkened to indigo. She rested her hand on his arm, feeling the warmth of his skin through his thin shirt. 'Then perhaps it's time you did.'

His voice was so low she had to strain to catch the words. 'If I don't tell someone, I think I'll go mad. ...' She waited patiently, and finally he began to speak, slowly and with difficulty at first, then more easily as he slipped back into the past. 'In the eyes of the world, Gerald Bowen was my father just as he was Greg's. He's been dead for five years now, and they say you shouldn't speak ill of the dead, but you know, Sharon, he hated me from the day I was born, and I'm still reaping the effects of that hate. I never knew my mother—she died shortly after I was born—but I've seen photos of her and read some of her letters, and a woman of warmth and sensitivity comes across the gap of all those years. But Gerald ... how would I describe him? Ambitious, fiercely competitive, with a genius for making money and an absolute ruthlessness towards anyone who got in his way. A cold man with a contempt for emotion, yet very possessive of anyone or anything he considered to be his. He and Alicia, my mother, were only married for a year when Greg was born—the son he'd wanted to carry on his little empire. This is pure speculation, but I think as the years passed Gerald must have killed off all the love and joy that my mother was capable of; he was angry, I know, that no more sons followed Greg.'

Ross threw away the mutilated piece of grass, plucking another one and beginning just as methodically to shred it to pieces. 'Perhaps what followed was inevitable. My mother met another man and they became lovers, but when she asked Gerald for a divorce he refused, even though she eventually told him she was pregnant by her lover, not by her husband. She'd left home by then, and I'd like to think she could have remarried sooner or later ... but before she could, her lover—my real father—was killed in a plane crash. She bore me, came back to Gerald, and died three months later—officially of pneumonia, unofficially, I would imagine, of a broken heart. Outwardly I was brought up as Gerald's son and Greg's brother; but I suppose to Gerald I was the living symbol of his wife's betrayal, and he managed to poison Greg's mind against me too, so that in some way I became the one to blame for Alicia's death. . . .'

Behind this brief summary Sharon sensed a childhood that must have been filled with loneliness and a bewildering lack of love, and her heart was filled with compassion for him. But he was speaking again. . . . 'Gerald bought Marshwinds years ago when I was a teenager. He got it cheaply because it was so run-down, so for him it was a business deal, a good investment. He had no interest in farming whatsoever. But I started spending weekends out here—he'd hired a farm manager, you see—and that's when the love affair with the place began. It's gone on ever since. I went to agricultural college in Guelph and as soon as I graduated I took over the farm. Then five years ago Gerald died . . . we hadn't seen that much of each other since I started coming out to Marshwinds, and I guess I'd hoped the old hostility and anger had somehow died down. At the reading of his will I found out differently.' He crumpled up the little ball of grass and flung it away, staring out over the river. 'He left Marshwinds to Greg with the proviso that it must be sold within five years. I have the first option—but Greg can ask whatever price he likes. If I don't buy it, then it goes to someone else.' His voice was flat. 'The reason Greg came out today was to tell me he's set the price: three-quarters of a million dollars, which I have to produce by the end of the summer. He knows as well as I do that I haven't got a chance of coming anywhere near that figure. The farm pays its way and gives me a decent salary, but it won't be a big money-making venture for a few years yet, and with interest rates the way they are, I can't afford to borrow the money. So the place will be sold out from under me.'

Sharon must have made some sound of distress, because he glanced over at her. 'You haven't heard the worst yet, he said bitterly. 'Gerald must have really enjoyed making up his will. Eight years from the time of his death—three years from now—I inherit a sizeable chunk of his fortune, enough to buy back Marshwinds three times over. But by then it will be too late. . . .'

Appalled, she whispered, 'How he must have hated you!'

'Oh, yes ... no doubt of that. And Greg's inherited that hatred—he's going to love seeing me turned out of the only place that's ever seemed like home to me. And there's not one thing I can do to stop him.'

She was holding his arm again, trying through the touch of her hand to give him what small solace she could. 'It's not possible to fight the will?'

'Afraid not. Gerald hired the best lawyers in the province to make sure there'd be no loopholes.' He suddenly seemed to become aware of her fingers on his sleeve. Glancing down, he rested his own hand on top of hers, giving it a little squeeze. 'Don't look so upset, Sharon—I shouldn't have burdened you with all this, it wasn't very fair of me.' He smiled with a touch of genuine warmth, a smile that inexplicably made her want to cry. 'You must be a good listener.'

'There's really nothing you can do?' she asked helplessly.

'In three years' time I'll be in a position to buy another place——'

'But it won't be Marshwinds.'

'No, it won't be Marshwinds.'

She shivered, and almost instinctively, it seemed, his arm went around her shoulders. 'You're cold—we'd better go back.' His arm tightened. 'Thank you, Sharon.'

She smiled mutely, knowing what was going to happen and welcoming it with all her heart. His kiss began gently, a simple expression of gratitude, and trustingly she responded, offering him a comfort that needed no words. But somehow they caught fire from each other. His mouth began moving against hers with an urgency and an unspoken demand that intoxicated her, obliterating all sense of caution or restraint. His hands were tangled in the smooth weight of her hair, holding her a willing prisoner, as she boldly ran her palms up his chest to hold him by the shoulders, feeling with a primitive thrill of delight the curve of bone and muscle; it made her very much aware of how much larger he was than she, how differently made: male to her female.

His mouth left hers to slide down the sweet-scented skin of her throat to the hollow at its base; from the hammering of her pulse he must have divined her excitement, from the pliancy of her body her willingness for his caresses. His hand found the soft swell of her breast under her thin blouse; the shock rippled through her body and she made a tiny sound of mingled protest and pleasure. 'You want this as much as I do, don't you, Sharon?' he muttered against her throat, rhythmically stroking her breast while he spoke. 'I've wanted you ever since I first saw you in the barn that night with your long hair, black as a witch's, your eyes like flower petals.'

Sharon had never felt anything to compare with the sweet ache of desire that flooded her whole being, imperative in its demands, in only a few seconds banishing the innocence of years, the ignorance of her unawakened body. When she felt him undo the buttons of her shirt and then the front closure of her bra, it was with a shudder of anticipation, while the sight of his long, lean fingers cupping her flesh made hot colour rush to her face. 'Ross . . .' she murmured, not even knowing herself if she was begging him to stop or to do more.

He had pushed her shirt away from her body, exposing her breasts to the moonlight, the skin pale as marble. 'You're so beautiful,' he said huskily. His eyes wandering over her body with an open possessiveness that made her tremble, he began unbuttoning his shirt, then his hands moved to his belt buckle. 'Take your clothes off, Sharon—we don't want to wait any longer, do we?'

His words and his actions struck a chord of terror deep within her, banishing the magic of his touch as if it had never been. 'Wait for what?' she said stupidly.

He leaned forward and kissed her, laughingly indulgently. 'I want to make love to you. Here and now. With only the moon to watch us. And you want it too, don't you?'

'No!' she gasped. 'No, Ross, I——' She broke off, for his hands had found her breasts again, stroking her skin with fire, making a mockery of her frantic denial. With the last vestige of her willpower she struck his hands away and pulled back from him fumbling with the fastenings on her blouse. 'Please ... you mustn't——'

His face had hardened. 'Come off it, Sharon. Who are you trying to kid?'

Trying to gather her wits, she stammered, 'No one. But I can't make love to you——'

'Why not?' he demanded. 'Give me one good reason.'

'I don't even know you! I only met you a week ago.'

'That's got nothing to do with it, you know that as well as I do. Let's quit fooling ourselves—we're two adults, we want each other, there's nothing to stop us.'

'You make it sound so cold-blooded. So—so practical,' she remonstrated.

'I'm not going to pretend to be in love with you, if that's what you mean,' he said with brutal honesty. 'Anyway, Sharon, why the terrified virgin act? It's hardly necessary, I would have thought.'

Her chin snapped up. 'Now just what do you mean by that?'

'I mean you're no more a virgin than I am.'

'I can't speak for you,' she retorted angrily. 'But I can for me—and it so happens I *am* a virgin, Ross Bowen. And for now, at any rate, I intend to stay that way!'

His hand was gripping her wrist. 'I don't believe you.'

'That's your problem!'

'The first time I saw you, I knew what you were like—rootless, drifting, going where the good times are and taking whatever comes along. Men, drink, drugs—it's all one to you.'

She sensed in him the same repressed violence she had seen that first night in the barn; but tonight she was not wet and cold and too exhausted to put up a fight. She said bluntly, 'There are undoubtedly girls like that. But I don't happen to be one of them.'

'That's what you say.'

'Yes, Ross, that's what I say.'

Something in her straightforward manner must have impressed him. He said slowly, 'Then if you're not, who are you, Sharon? Tell me why you were hitchhiking on a lonely back road miles from anywhere. Tell me why you left Montreal ... what you were running away from.'

Briefly she closed her eyes. Earlier he had shared with her his pain and frustration over the imminent loss of his beloved farm, and had given her glimpses of a childhood devoid of love and support. Dared she trust him with her own story?

'I'll tell you why I was hitchhiking,' she said quietly. 'That much, at least. . . .' She looped her arms around her knees, gazing out over the gleaming mud flats as she tried to decide where to begin. 'My whole life has been preoccupied with possessions and outward appearances. My father was a poet—not a very good poet, I'm afraid. But he thought he was good, far too good for the common crowd to appreciate him, and my mother bolstered him in that belief. He had an inherited income, large enough that he had never had to sully himself with real work, too small to furnish him with the kind of life-style he would have liked or with the front he wanted to present to all his academic and literary friends. So my mother dedicated her whole life to preserving that front: the gracious, intellectual life where money was unimportant and art was everything.' Sharon paused, surprised to hear so much bitterness in her voice; for so many years she had schooled herself to keep her thoughts to herself, that sharing them now was a kind of catharsis.

'I was their only child,' she went on. 'So it was inevitable, I suppose, that I got caught up in it. I was also the only really practical one in the family. I learned very early to turn the cushion covers so they looked like new, and to move the furniture around so the worn places on the rug didn't show. I learned how to cook gourmet meals on a shoestring and how to scrimp on family meals so we could afford to give an elegant little cocktail party for all the right people. I got jobs as soon as I was old enough, and I always paid my parents part of my salary because they couldn't have managed without it. Not that they ever thanked me—I think they thought it was their due.' She rested her forehead on her knees. 'I'm sorry—I sound mean and bitter, don't I? But it was all so fake, Ross, so unreal. And for what? To impress people who, in my estimation, weren't worth impressing.' Looking up, her face strained, she said, 'Do you understand what I mean? Or am I not making any sense at all?'

He rested a hand on her shoulder, where it lay warm and heavy, and very comforting. 'Of course I understand. When I asked you why you wanted the job here, you said the farm was so beautiful and yet so rooted in reality—it must have seemed the exact opposite of your parents' house.'

Strangely pleased that he had remembered what she had said, and pleased also by his discernment, she said warmly, 'Exactly! There's nothing fake about a farm, is there? It's useful and real, and there's no time or energy for show or pretence.'

'Hardly,' he agreed drily. Hesitating a little, he added, 'And your parents? You spoke of them in the past tense.'

'Yes. They died last December, in a car crash. They were on their way to a literary convention in Toronto, and rather than travel on the bus with everyone else, they took the car. It was old, and needed repairs. One of the tires blew on the expressway, and that was that.' In spite of herself, her voice quivered.

'I'm sorry,' he said simply.

'Mmm. . . .' She blinked back the tears that always came when she thought of her handsome, impractical father, and her mother's artificial gaiety and warmth; as she, Sharon, had grown older it was almost as if the roles had reversed and they had been the children and she the parent. 'Anyway,' she continued valiantly, 'you see why I like hitchhiking. The only possessions are those I carry on my back. No house, no furniture, no people—only me.'

A silence fell. Ross's hand was still on her shoulder,

nor did she want him to move it. She was not a girl normally given to confidences; Joan had known of her family problems, of course, but for some reason she had not shared them with Roger. For the first time it occurred to her to wonder why not. Perhaps because subconsciously she had realised he placed a similar importance on outward appearances? A suspicion that was later fully justified, she thought grimly.

'And what of the rest, Sharon?' Ross said quietly. 'What made you decide to leave Montreal—the loss of your parents?'

She looked past him, the moonlight making of her features a cameo in black and white. She could lie to him, for he had given her the perfect opening to do so. 'No, it wasn't that.' The silence stretched out. 'I can't tell you,' she said finally with a helpless shrug of her shoulders. 'It's—I just can't.' It had been too horrible, too much of a nightmare from which she had not yet awoken. . . .

'You don't trust me?' His fingers were digging into her arm and she shifted uncomfortably. 'Is that it?'

She could feel the whole force of his personality directed at her, strong and implacable, and suddenly she shivered. 'I don't know,' she said in a low voice, and it was the absolute truth. 'It takes time to build up trust.'

It was an answer that obviously did not satisfy him. 'Try me,' he said uncompromisingly. 'I promise to give you a fair hearing.'

But would he? All too clearly she could recall his murderous responses whenever the subject of drugs had come up, and somehow she could not bear to reveal to him the whole sorry, sordid story, a story that, moreover, lacked a proper ending: it would have to be left hanging in the air, the culprit neither exonerated nor found guilty. 'I can't, Ross!' she blurted. 'I just can't.' Once again her head dropped to her knee. 'I'm sorry.'

'So am I,' he said with the clarity of extreme anger. 'You're an intelligent woman, Sharon, so you must see where this leaves me. Suspecting the worst, of course.

Because otherwise why won't you tell me what happened? Why you've been running away?'

Yet if she were to tell him the truth, plain and unadorned, he would also suspect the worst, she thought wretchedly. 'I'm cold,' she muttered. 'I'd like to go back.'

'Go ahead,' he said indifferently. 'You can see the house from here, you'll have no trouble finding your way.'

'Aren't you coming?'

'No.'

She found she was staring downwards into the depths of the channel; the tide had turned and almost visibly the water was creeping up the bank, mud-churned and absolutely silent in its advance. Sinister and deadly. A person could drown in it and never be found. 'Ross, you wouldn't——'

'I just want to be alone, Sharon,' he said with barely disguised impatience.

Alone to worry about Marshwinds . . . knowing there was nothing, absolutely nothing, she could say or do to help except to remove herself from his presence, she got to her feet. The light on the water that earlier had radiated a haunting beauty now merely seemed cold and unfriendly, a fit accompaniment to the kind of loneliness and despair Ross must be feeling. She had never felt so helpless in her life, so totally cut off from another human being. 'Please, Ross——' she began.

'Go home, Sharon,' he said, not even bothering to look up at her. 'We've got nothing to give each other. I thought for a while perhaps we did—but I was wrong.'

He had put into words a feeling she herself had had, and for some reason this seemed the final straw. She turned on her heel and began walking away from him down the slope of the dyke, the long grass rustling with every step. Her eyes resolutely on the ground, her hands thrust into the pockets of her jeans, she tramped on, and the small hope that he would call her back died a slow death as the distance between them increased. Even when she knew he must be out of sight she kept up the same steady pace, her only accompaniment the stark black outline of her own shadow on the pale grass.

It seemed to take a long time to reach the farmhouse, but finally she did. Letting herself in, she went straight to her room and closed the door, drawing the curtains across the window to shut out the false peace of the moonlit night. Although she craved the oblivion of sleep, it was a long time in coming, nor before she finally dropped off to sleep did she hear the sound she had been listening for: the fall of Ross's steps along the hall past her door.

CHAPTER FOUR

IF Sharon had thought she was working hard the first few days at the farm, the haying season was to show her what real work was. It was late June by now, and the first crop was ready to be mowed and baled on the dykes; despite all the modern equipment, it was still an operation very much dependent on the weather, so as the hot, dry days succeeded one another, the work proceeded at a frenetic pace. It would have been manageable if everything else could have stopped, Sharon soon decided, but the cows still had to be brought in from the pasture and milked, the barn cleaned, the heifers fed, until she wondered how there could be enough hours in the day to fit everything in, let alone enough energy to do it all.

Ross worked like a man possessed, as if by sheer hard labour he could exorcise the threat that hung over him and over Marshwinds; Sharon had never been afraid of hard work, but she soon found she could not possibly keep up with him, for he seemed to draw on reserves of strength and willpower far beyond her own. She might not like the way he treated her as a woman, or the way he seemed intent upon docketing her as promiscuous and even criminal in her behaviour, but she could not help but admire his drive and energy, and the unflagging good humour with which he dealt with the farmhands.

Day by day the bales accumulated in the high lofts of the dairy barn and the heifer barn, until they were counting them in thousands rather than hundreds; and day by day the sun continued to shine. Sharon had by now more or less taken over the dairy operations singlehandedly, leaving Ross free to go to the fields at dawn and work there until dark. When her chores were done, she would help the haying crew by throwing the rectangular bales from the slatted carts on to the loader that carried them up into the barn on a moving conveyor belt, or by removing them at the upper end and stacking them in piles—hard, backbreaking labour that left her hot, dusty, and tired to the point of exhaustion by nightfall.

That the strain was also beginning to tell on Ross was easy enough to see. By evening his eyes were dark-circled, sunk in their sockets, while the skin of his face, stretched tight over his cheekbones, took on a greyish tinge under his tan; he fell asleep as he sat at the supper table one night, his chin drooping to lie on his chest, his lashes as thick as a girl's on his cheeks, so that Sharon had to swallow a surge of compassion, intense enough to frighten her. As he jolted himself awake, automatically starting to eat again, she forced herself to concentrate on her food, knowing that her sympathy was the last thing he would want.

By eleven o'clock the next morning, Sharon knew it was going to be one of those days when she would have been better off staying in bed. When she had rounded up the cows in the pasture and had guided them into their stalls in the barn, she discovered she was one short, which necessitated a return trip to the meadow. Since by now a number of the cows had developed definite personalities in her eyes, she was not at all surprised to find that the missing cow was Myrtle, a long-lashed Guernsey who was coyly hiding herself among a group of yearlings. I thought you'd never come for me, Myrtle seemed to be saying, as Sharon crossly shooed her up towards the gate, the herd of yearlings following hard on their heels, insatiably curious. It was another hot day, with unusually not even a hint of a cooling breeze off the basin; the dykes shimmered in the heat, and far to her right she could see the haying crew at work in one of the fields and hear the distant mutter of the machinery.

Because she was in a hurry, everything seemed to take twice as long as usual, and it was her own carelessness that caused the next contretemps. Ross had warned her about the Holstein who went by the unlikely name of Melanie: watch her, he had said to Sharon on her very first day in the barn. She kicks. But today, because Sharon was rushed, she plunked herself down beside Melanie without her usual caution. The rear hind leg lashed out, the protruding knob of bone catching her on the bridge of the nose. She fell back, stifling a cry of pain, involuntary tears filling her eyes. Although she went immediately to the pump room and applied cold water to her face, by the time she had finished milking her flesh was swollen and discoloured, painful to the touch.

She led the cows back to the pasture, closing the gate behind them, and then trailed back up the slope to the barn. It was unbearably hot in the pump room, her jeans sticking to her legs, her T-shirt damp with perspiration. She had just finished washing all the equipment and was rinsing out the big stainless steel sink when the door burst open.

'You must have left the gate open!' Ross accused her furiously. 'The cows are out. Leave that and help me round them up.'

'I know I latched it,' she protested.

'You couldn't have,' he said shortly. 'I'd have thought by now you could have been a little more careful.'

He was striding across the yard and she had to run to keep up with him. 'I latched the gate, Ross Bowen,' she said with the icy clarity of extreme anger.

'Then how the hell did they get out?'

'I have no idea,' she retorted breathlessly, adding in

dismay, 'Oh no, look at them—they're all through the orchard!'

'I can't afford the time for this,' Ross said grimly. 'For goodness' sake watch what you're doing from now on, okay?'

It was too much. Sharon stopped dead in her tracks, stamping her foot in an exhilarating rush of pure rage. 'I won't go one step further until you apologise for that,' she seethed. 'It was *not* my fault!'

He turned to face her, a matching anger blazing in his blue eyes, his hands clenched to fists at his sides. 'Whose was it, then?' he demanded. His voice altered. 'What happened to your face?'

'Melanie kicked me.'

If she had hoped for sympathy, she was soon disappointed. 'I warned you about that, too,' he said impatiently.

'It must be nice to be as perfect as you,' she snapped, knowing she was being childish but unable to prevent herself. 'Don't you ever make mistakes?'

'I sure do,' was the swift retort. 'Like the day I hired you, for instance.'

As she flinched away from him, the last vestige of anger driven away by hurt that he could say such a thing, a man's voice shouted to them from the orchard. Ross glanced over his shoulder. 'Doug and Mike are already over there—we'd better go.'

As they rounded up the cows from among the apple trees, driving them back through the gate into the pasture, Sharon kept her distance from Ross, her mind preoccupied with the way he had lashed out at her so unfairly; it seemed to indicate that his initial dislike of her had in no way ameliorated. He still thought of her as careless and irresponsible, a handicap rather than a help. As she cautiously tapped Melanie on the rump with a stick to encourage her to join the rest, Sharon felt tears blur her vision. Why Ross Bowen's opinion of her should matter so much, she did not know; but it was horribly apparent that it did.

Finally the last cow—Myrtle, of course—sauntered through the gate, and Sharon rather ostentatiously stood back so that Ross could slide the chain onto the convoluted metal catch that held the gate shut. Doug and Mike had gone. She said flatly, 'I have a couple of things to do at the barn. Then I'll help with the hay.'

He straightened, the sunlight mercilessly delineated the fatigue in his face. 'I owe you an apology, Sharon,' he said quietly. 'The cows got through the fence up at the north-west corner. Doug told me—he's up there fixing it now.' He ran his fingers through his thick, untidy hair. 'I'm sorry I yelled at you. And I'm sorry I jumped to all the wrong conclusions.'

A weight seemed to be lifting from her shoulders. But there was one more thing she needed to know. Her violet eyes wary, she asked, '*Are* you sorry you hired me, Ross?'

He stepped closer. His shirt was dirty, she noticed abstractedly, grimed with dust and with wisps of hay adhering to it. 'No. I shouldn't have said that either, because it's not true.' He rested his hands on her shoulders, a new weight that she welcomed. 'You're a good worker, Sharon. You've learned an incredible amount since you came here, you're reliable and intelligent and more than willing to do your fair share. I don't know why I said that—it hurt you, didn't it?'

She nodded slowly. 'Yes, it did.'

'I'm sorry.'

She smiled, and said with a lightness that was partly feigned, 'You're forgiven.'

He squeezed her gently before releasing her. 'It must be just about time for a coffee. Then why don't you come down to the dykes with me on the truck? I want to check the baler.' He grinned ruefully. 'A change is as good as a rest, they say.'

'I'd like that.' With a sharp pang she knew that had he kissed her then, she would have welcomed it; but he made no move to do so. They walked up to the house together, talking about the weather forecast and last week's exceptionally high milk yield, nice safe topics that bore very little relation to the confusion in Sharon's mind. One thing she did know: Ross Bowen was a man unlike any other she had ever met. Certainly as different from Roger as a man could be. Roger, even though not yet thirty, had already been gaining a reputation in the Montreal hospital where she had worked as a brilliant diagnostician—the man to call in when all the tests had failed to pinpoint a patient's illness. And ninety-nine times out of a hundred he would be right. As she preceded Ross into the back porch, she decided that being right had been very important to Roger, whether it was related to his work or to his personal life. Somehow she could not imagine Roger apologising for a mistake as straightforwardly as Ross had done, for that would mean admitting he had been wrong, and Roger would find that very difficult to do, if not impossible. . . .

Jock put a mug of coffee on the table for her as well as a huge piece of generously buttered coffee cake which she attacked with gusto: it was a long time since breakfast. Ross had pulled off his shirt and was sluicing water over his face and neck at the sink; his back was deeply tanned, the muscles rippling under the skin, his spine a long curve. Hurriedly, before he could turn around and catch her staring, she buried her face in her coffee mug. He dried his face and arms and sat down across from her, moisture still caught in the tangled mat of blond hair on his chest, and again it was an effort for her not to stare. Darn the man, she thought crossly. Why did he have this effect on her? It was not as if she was a starstruck teenager, after all. And she had seen plenty of male bodies in her years at the hospital. Why then this urge to run her fingers through his damp hair, to smooth the broad line of his shoulders and massage the strong column of his neck? She had never felt this way with Roger, or indeed with anyone else.

It was almost a relief when they got up from the table and went back out into the porch. 'I think that's a clean shirt on the hook there,' Ross said casually. 'Pass it to me, will you, please?'

She took it down from the wall and was about to give it to him when she noticed an immense black spider running along the collar only inches from her hand. With a shriek of alarm she flung the shirt from her,

taking an involuntary step backwards and colliding
with the hard wall of Ross's chest. In a reflex action his
arms went around her.

She shuddered. 'Ugh! Did you see that? I'm terrified
of spiders!'

She could feel the laughter rumble in his chest. 'I
never would have guessed!'

'That night in the barn I was scared to death one
would run across my face,' she confessed, a glint of
humour in her eyes as she looked up at him. For some
reason he had not removed his arms; she discovered
that she liked being held by him very much, liked the
way he was smiling down at her, his deep blue eyes
steady on her face.

'You're a strange mixture, Sharon Reid. You got rid
of Steve, who's twice your size, in short order—but a
spider makes you run for cover.'

'If you were a male chauvinist, you'd call that a
typically female lack of logic,' she said provocatively.

'Heaven forbid,' he said piously. 'Will you let go of
me now, so that I can get my shirt?'

'I'm not holding on to you!' she retorted spiritedly.
'It's the other way around.'

'Is it now? So it is. . . .' Something that was not
laughter flashed through his eyes. 'I wonder how that
happened,' he murmured before lowering his head to
kiss her.

Sharon stood very still in the circle of his arms. His
lips were confident of their welcome, moving slowly and
surely against her own, while through her thin shirt she
could feel the warmth and hardness of his body; his
skin smelled of soap and hay, tantalisingly masculine.
Shyly she slid her hands up his chest, feeling the
roughness of hair, the tautness of muscle, the hard
curve of rib bone, and she was suffused with the strange
sensation that she had come home, that her whole life
had been leading up to this one perfect moment.

Very slowly he released her. Her eyes were full of
wonderment, the pulse at her throat fluttering against
the skin. 'You're an enigma, Sharon,' he said huskily.
'I'm pulled to you—Oh, how I'm pulled to you! Yet at

the same time I'm so aware of all the things you haven't told me—won't tell me. So I'm pushed away at the same time.' His arms dropped to his sides as with a deliberate change of subject he added, 'We'd better go. It's time I relieved Mike on the baler.' He bent to retrieve his shirt, shaking it first before putting it on. 'Ready?'

She nodded mutely, quite unable to think of a thing to say. When he had let go of her, she had felt bereft, so much so that she was frightened. There was no place in her life for Ross Bowen, with his suspicions and lack of trust; she did not need them any more than she had needed Roger's defection. As they went outside she saw Wolf lying in the shade of the lilac bushes and gratefully seized on him as a topic of conversation. 'Is Wolf a Siberian husky?'

'No, a Malemute. He used to be a sled dog up north. He's useless in the hot weather because his coat stays far too thick for comfort. So he spends half the summer digging great holes in the lawn trying to get down to the permafrost.'

'You're kidding!'

'I wish I were,' Ross responded drily. Wolf's tail waved lackadaisically as they walked past, although he did not bother raising his shaggy black head. 'He's happiest when it's thirty below and snowing a blizzard. The rest of the year he doesn't even earn his keep. If he were any good at all, he would have been out rounding up the cows for us this morning.'

They got into the truck and Ross turned down the narrow dirt road that led to the dykes. Curious to learn a little more about Ross rather than about Wolf, Sharon asked, 'Why do you keep him, then?'

His face closed. 'Oh, he belonged to someone who was—who's dead now. The corn's growing well, isn't it?'

In other words, mind your own business, Sharon, she thought wryly, making an appropriate reply. Followed by a cloud of brown dust, they drove about half a mile over the meadowland before Ross turned on to a dirt track that bumped its way across the field towards the tractor and baler. Doug, a dour, black-haired man who always seemed to look through Sharon rather than at her, was driving the tractor, while Mike balanced on the platform behind the baler, shoving the bales to the ground in heaps of four. He was younger, blond-haired and pleasant-faced, with a timid little wife named Doris whom he adored; Sharon had met her a week or so ago, and had been touched by his protective attitude towards her.

Even as they watched, Mike yelled something at Doug, who slowed the tractor to a halt. Ross turned off the truck and the growl of the tractor's engine sounded very loud on the hot summer air. 'Something's jammed,' Ross said tersely. 'I wonder if he turned the drive shift off.'

Mike had jumped off the platform and was bent over the baler, tugging at something. Sharon got out of the truck, aware of a faint sense of unease, aware too that Ross had followed her example and was striding across the grass behind her. As if in slow motion, she saw Mike's body suddenly jerked into the machine, heard his thin scream of agony, saw Doug swivel in the tractor seat, his face a rictus of horror. The tractor motor was turned off. Incongruously high and sweet, a bobolink carolled its song into the silence.

Instinctively Sharon had begun running the instant it had happened; she was the first to reach Mike. He was bent over the baler, his face paper-white, as he watched a steady stream of blood pump from the deep gash in his arm to drip on the ground. Taking command without even thinking as she slipped into a long-familiar role, she said crisply to Ross, 'Lay him flat and give me your shirt.' It had taken only a split second for her to realise what had happened: one of the long, pointed metal teeth on the baler pick-up had caught in the sleeve of Mike's shirt and had ripped the whole length of his arm open. Arterial blood, she thought swiftly, pressing the garment Ross had passed her firmly on the wound. 'Hold it there,' she said briefly, with her fingers locating the pressure point for the artery; almost immediately the flow of blood slowed.

'We'll have to get him to a hospital, Ross—what's the quickest way to do that?'

'I'd better call an ambulance. Doug and I will go up to the house. I'll leave Doug there to direct them down here, and I'll come back as soon as I've phoned.'

'Is there anything I can cover him with? He's in shock—he should be kept warm.'

'There's a blanket in the truck.'

As Sharon kept pressure on the wound, Ross wrapped what looked like an old army blanket around Mike's supine body. 'I'll be back in a few minutes.'

Sharon knelt at Mike's side, her eyes noting the pallor and clamminess of his skin, the dazed look in his eyes. 'They've gone for an ambulance,' she said to him calmly. 'You're going to be all right.'

'Doris,' he said thickly. 'Will someone tell Doris?'

'Yes, I'll look after that.'

Her steadiness seemed to reassure him, for his eyelids drooped shut. She stayed quietly by his side, knowing there was nothing more she could do for him; in what seemed like a very short time she heard the rattle of the truck approaching, and soon Ross was kneeling beside her. 'Ambulance should be here in ten or fifteen minutes. How is he?'

'I think he'll be all right. He'll have to have an operation, because there's a lot of torn tissue—I just hope the nerves weren't damaged,' she said in a low voice. 'He's worried about Doris.'

'I'll go and see her once the ambulance has come—I could run her into the hospital. She's a nice little thing. . . Mike used to be a pretty wild kid, but since he met Doris, he's settled right down.'

Mike stirred restlessly, muttering something under his breath. Sharon put a hand on his forehead, where the skin was cold and clammy, hoping the ambulance was on its way. The minutes passed slowly; it seemed like a long time until Ross stood up, saying abruptly, 'That looks like it coming now.'

She glanced over her shoulder, seeing the ambulance like a tiny speck on the far side of the dykes, its red lights winking. Mike seemed to have lapsed into unconsciousness, his pulse slower than it had been. She stayed where she was as Ross walked towards the road to flag the ambulance down; it drove over the stubbled grass and came to a halt, the back doors swinging open as a white-uniformed young man jumped down and pulled a long metal-framed stretcher out of the back. The driver joined him and they wheeled it across the grass.

From the name tag on his pocket, Sharon realised the first man was an intern. Crisply she described to him what had happened, and gave her estimation of Mike's injuries. The intern did a quick examination. 'You did well,' he said briefly. 'You minimised the blood loss, and that's the most important thing. Should be no problem.' Meanwhile Ross had been giving Mike's name and age to the driver, explaining that he was going to inform Mike's wife of the accident. In short order Mike was eased on to the stretcher and loaded into the ambulance, which then reversed away from the tractor and drove off as fast as the state of the roads would allow.

Sharon watched it go, feeling suddenly very tired now that she was released from the responsibility for Mike's welfare. She stretched to relieve the tension in her muscles, rubbing at the back of her neck.

'Were you a doctor or a nurse?'

Her eyes flew to Ross's face. There had been a vicious edge to his voice, warning her that she was in trouble. His eyes were ice-cold, by sheer force of will demanding a response from her. For the first time since she had seen Mike dragged into the machine, she realised how blatantly she had betrayed herself: her decisiveness, her skill at stopping the bleeding, her instant command of the situation, must all have spoken volumes to Ross. Yet how could she have done otherwise? She pushed back a strand of hair from her face, leaving a streak of blood on her cheek. 'I'm a nurse.'

'You *were* a nurse.'

No mercy in those cold blue eyes. 'Very well,' she said with a dignity that became her. 'I was a nurse.'

'Were you fired?'

She felt the first stirrings of anger and her chin lifted defiantly. 'No.'

'So you resigned—why?'

'I don't really see that it's any of your business.'

'I'm making it my business, Sharon—and we're not leaving here until I get a few answers.'

'You have to go and see Doris.'

'In that case,' he said unpleasantly, 'you'd better hurry up and tell me what I want to know, hadn't you?' An ugly emphasis on every word, he repeated, 'Why did you resign, Sharon? It was something to do with drugs, wasn't it? There are lots of those in a hospital. . . .'

Deep within her something snapped. She took a step towards him, her hands on her hips, twin patches of colour in her cheeks that a moment ago had been pale with fatigue. 'All right, I'll tell you,' she blazed. 'And then if *you* want to fire me, you can. . . . I was only nineteen when I graduated from nursing school, a brilliant student, they said, you should have a brilliant future.' Briefly her voice wavered. 'I went to work right away and I loved every minute of it—it was practical, it was real, I was of use. It was the antidote I needed for my home life. The administration must have thought I was of use, too, because last year I was appointed head nurse for my station on the men's surgical ward—which meant, among other things, that I had the responsibility for the drug cupboard for the whole floor.'

As clearly as if she was standing there, she could see the immaculately tidy store room with its piles of clean linen, its stacks of boxed equipment, its locked drug cupboard to which she alone of all the nursing staff had had the key. 'Early in February there was a massive theft of drugs from that cupboard. Amphetamines, barbiturates, hallucinogens, the works. I discovered it first thing in the morning, so it must have happened on the night shift. . . .'

She was looking past Ross now, almost as if she had forgotten he was there, her eyes fixed unseeingly on the distant line of hills. 'My fingerprints were all over the cupboard, of course—and no one else's. I was the one with the key. And unfortunately that night I had paid a visit to one of the patients on my floor, an elderly man who had had to have a leg amputated, and who wanted someone to talk to. So I'd dropped in around eight that evening and stayed for over an hour.' Her voice devoid of expression she went on, 'There was an inquiry, of course—a private one, run by the hospital board. During the course of the inquiry they found out about all the debts that my parents had left after they died. So I had the means, the opportunity, the motive. The only thing they couldn't find was the drugs themselves, or whether I'd received any large sums of money from selling them. So eventually the case was dropped for lack of sufficient evidence. After that, they couldn't fire me, of course. I stayed on for three months—a matter of pride, I guess.' Unconsciously her fingers were twisting and untwisting themselves around her belt, the only outward signs of an inward conflict. 'It was dreadful. They say in this country you're innocent until proven guilty. That may be true in theory, but it sure doesn't work in practice. A hospital is such a closed little world, and of course everyone knew about the theft and the results of the inquiry—I think most of them thought I'd done it and had been lucky enough to get away with it . . . I stuck it out until the end of May, and shortly afterwards I left Montreal.' She shrugged. 'The rest you know.'

'And did you do it. Sharon?'

Slowly her eyes travelled back to his face. In his expression she saw the same coldness, the same frightening objectivity that had been in that array of faces at the inquiry. Impassive. Withholding judgment. Unmoved by her one passionate plea of innocence when she had broken through the rigid judicial procedures and had sworn with all the intensity of her nature that she had had nothing to do with the theft, that it was the last thing on God's earth that she would have been likely to have done. . . . Standing very straight, she said evenly, 'Ross, why do you ask that? Either you think I'm innocent or guilty. If you think I'm innocent, you don't need to ask. If you think I'm guilty, will my denying it change your mind?'

'I don't know what to think,' he said heavily.

She must have been hoping that, having heard her story, he would believe in her innocence, for his prevarication came as a bitter blow. She said coldly, 'So you want me to leave Marshwinds?'

'No. With Mike out of commission, I can't afford to lose anyone else.'

It was not what one could call a gesture of faith. Determined that he should not see how much he had hurt her, she took refuge in anger. 'Thanks a lot!' she snapped.

'What did you expect—some kind of a testimonial?' he retorted with a matching anger.

Perhaps she had—but be damned if she'd tell him that. 'Hardly—from the very beginning you've taken great pleasure in thinking the worst of me.' Recklessly she flung the words at him. 'Why, Ross? Why do you overreact every time the word drugs comes up? Were you hooked on them once yourself? Is that it?'

If she had been seeking a reaction from him, she had more than succeeded. She fought the urge to retreat as he took two steps towards her, gripping her by the shoulders, in his eyes the same murderous rage that she remembered all too well from their first encounter. 'Let me tell you why I overreact, as you succinctly put it. Five or six years after my mother died, Gerald remarried—a nice safe marriage to a woman without looks or personality, who was, besides, healthily scared of him. Some years later she presented him with a son— my half-brother, I suppose, although it's hard to sort out relationships in my family, isn't it?' She shrank back from the savagery in his voice. 'Peter was his name. He was a nice kid, not a mean bone in his body. Went through life thinking the best of everyone, and very often finding it. I liked him—I used to spend a lot of time with him. He was certainly the only one of my family who ever came anywhere near understanding my attachment to Marshwinds.'

His voice rough with emotion, Ross went on, 'If he had a fault it was that he was too easily led, too naïve to believe anyone would wilfully harm him. Last summer, the summer he was eighteen, he got in with the wrong crowd. The kids who didn't have jobs but always seemed to have plenty of money, and who had nothing better to do than have a good time. A whole group of them took off hitchhiking to Cape Breton, to go camping there. If he'd been my son, I wouldn't have allowed him to go, but Emma, my stempmother, thought it would be a nice holiday for him, and Greg, of course, supported her. So off he went. . . .'

'What happened, Ross?' Sharon whispered, suffering the cruel grip of his fingers in her flesh because she already knew that Peter was dead and that his death was the source of all of Ross's pain and anger.

'The first evening they were there, they got Peter drunk—oh, I know you can't absolve him of responsibility, but I can just see him going along with it, thinking it was all in fun. Then they laced one of his drinks with drugs—a mixture of everything they'd got—and dared him to canoe across the lake. He tipped the canoe halfway over, and drowned.'

Sharon closed her eyes, visualising the scene all too clearly in her mind. 'No wonder you hate the very sound of the word drugs,' she whispered, more to herself than to him.

'I'm not through yet,' he said grimly. 'The police were never able to pinpoint who actually gave Peter the stuff—it could have been any one of ten of them, and of course none of them would admit to it. Lack of evidence, the police said. Innocent until proven guilty. So they all got off scot-free.'

'Just as I did,' she whispered, appalled by the parallels. 'So that's why you hate me!'

If she had been looking at him, she would have seen a flicker of emotion cross his features before he said levelly, 'That, at least, is why I find it hard to believe your story, or to trust in you. It's too close to what happened to Peter.'

She wanted to do nothing more than put her head on his shoulder and cry her eyes out—for Peter, for Ross, for herself. But she could not do that, not with a man who still believed her capable of stealing and lying. She moved back from him and his hands dropped to his sides. 'I understand,' she said with as much dignity as she could muster, knowing she had to change the subject: she could not bear much more of this emotional intensity. Glancing down at her watch, she added, 'Ross, we'd better go. It's important that you see Doris.'

He rubbed his forehead with the back of his hand, with a visible effort coming back to the present. 'Yeah . . . I'll drop you off at the house. Looks like you'll have to cope with the milking again, Sharon—sorry about that.'

That was the least of her worries, she thought with a desperate attempt at humour as the truck roared back towards the farm along the dry dirt road. As it turned out, it came as a relief to occupy herself with the routine chores in the dairy barn: its cool, dim atmosphere was soothing to her overstrained nerves, the placidity of the cows very comforting after so much anxiety and emotion. She could do nothing more for Mike other than hope he would suffer no permanent damage; she would phone the hospital when she went up to the house. As for Ross . . . as clearly as if he stood in front of her she could see the tamped-down rage in his eyes as he recounted Peter's tragic story, and she shivered as if the cold wings of death had brushed her. Ross . . . why should it matter so much what he thought of her? It seemed bitterly unfair that her ordeal in the Montreal hospital, that had already cost her so much, should continue to haunt her here, in a place so far away in space and time and so different in every way. Yet it was so . . . by one of those quirks of fate, she had ended up working for a man whose own past would compel him to disbelieve her and to hate the very association of her name with the theft of which she had been accused. Now that she knew about Peter, she could hardly blame him . . . although that realisation did nothing to lift the black cloud of depression that seemed to have settled over her. Ross was attracted to her, physically if in no other way, she knew that; yet at the same time he was repelled by the shadows in her past. Their relationship was like the tides, she decided fancifully, that were pulled high on the shore, then dragged back to the deep channels in the basin, up and down, back and forth, never still, controlled by forces beyond themselves.

When she finally trailed up to the house for supper, there was no sign of Ross. Jock was in the kitchen, and from the cool, shadowed recess under the long table, Wolf thumped his bushy tail on the floor in recognition of her arrival. Sharon pulled out a chair and sank down on it, wearily resting her chin on her hands.

'Quite a day, eh, miss?' Jock said sympathetically, filling the kettle and putting it on the stove. 'I phoned the hospital fifteen minutes ago, and the operation went well; by some miracle the brachial nerve was untouched, they said, so once the wound has healed, Mike should be as good as new. His wife is with him. Ross went back to the haying once he'd taken her there.'

'I'm so glad he's going to be all right—I was worried about nerve damage.' Jock had put a plate of ham and scalloped potatoes in front of her, with a side dish of salad, and she said gratefully, realising that it had been a very long time since she had eaten, 'Thanks, Jock. That looks lovely.'

Under the table Wolf nudged her foot, and impulsively she added, 'Ross once mentioned that Wolf had belonged to someone he knew—would it have been Peter?'

Jock had been putting glass dishes of pickles and chutney on the table in front of her; the tattooed serpents on his arms grew still as he answered slowly, 'Aye—Wolf was Peter's dog. Now how would you be knowing about Peter?'

She began to eat. 'Ross told me.'

'Did he now? It's not like thim to talk about Peter—the lad's death was a bitter blow for him, not something he talks about easily.'

She said hastily, with a diplomatic blend of truth and untruth, 'Maybe it was the stress of Mike's accident. Did you make this chutney yourself, Jock? It's delicious.'

'I did indeed.' Jock was not so easily deflected. 'I'm glad you're here, miss. Ross needs a bit of company, someone he can talk to. There's been little enough of that in his life.'

Unable to think of a simple reply to this, Sharon took a long drink of water and mumbled an indeterminate agreement. 'Will they be loading hay in the barn this evening, do you know?'

'I imagine so. The forecast is calling for rain, so Ross will want to get as many bales in as he can.'

'And because of Mike, we're short-handed—oh, dear!' She began to eat more quickly.

Afterwards, Sharon was to look back on that evening as an unadulterated nightmare. She was tired before she even left the house, for she had been up since five-thirty that morning and it had not been what one could call an easy day; besides, her nose was still sore, the blow having left her with a lingering headache. Her job was to stand in the hay wagon and throw the bales on to the conveyor belt that carried them up to the loft; she wore cotton gloves to protect her hands, but the muscles of her shoulders and arms were soon aching. Lift, heave, down ... lift, heave, down ... a never-ending rhythm. Too tired to think or even to assess how much more there was to do, she worked like an automaton, an extension of the machinery, her mind totally blank. One cart was emptied. Another took its place, and she began all over again. Lift, heave, down ... this time Ross was working with her, his only comment as he joined her a terse, 'They're loading up the last wagon down on the dykes—I can feel the rain coming, so we've got to get them in.'

She merely nodded, finding a small measure of relief in how much more quickly the wagon emptied with two people instead of one. As the final wagon was reversed into position she felt the first drops of rain on her overheated skin, and from somewhere she dredged up a fresh spurt of energy. Lift, heave, down; lift, heave, down ... in total silence she and Ross worked side by side. The rain was pattering on her bare arms and soaking through her thin shirt, spurring her to work faster. A dozen bales left. Six. Four. Two. And then there were none, she thought dazedly, pushing a strand of hair behind her ear. She straightened slowly, rubbing the small of her back. 'That's it,' she said with no great originality.

All too briefly Ross's hand rested on her shoulder. 'You worked your heart out, Sharon—thanks.'

She blinked up at him, too tired to even focus right; his face seemed to be wavering in and out of her field of vision. Then he was jumping down from the wagon and holding out his hand. 'Come on—time you went up to the house.'

She stumbled over the slatted floor towards him, reaching out her hand to grasp his; it was the only solid thing in a world that seemed to have lost its moorings, swaying up and down. She went to leap from the wagon to the ground, but somehow the ground was rushing up to meet her. She lost her balance, pitching forward, her last coherent memory of Ross's sudden lunge forward to catch her.

CHAPTER FIVE

IT was with a strange sense of history repeating itself that Sharon came to her senses in Ross's arms, being carried through the rain and the gathering darkness to the house. She did not have the strength for even a token struggle. Closing her eyes, she let her cheek rest against his chest; he smelled of sweat and hay, and she could feel the strong, steady beat of his heart.

She had a confused impression of lights and radio music as they went through the kitchen. The next sensation was of the softness of her mattress as she was lowered on to the bed in her room. Her head drooped to one side on the pillow. All she wanted to do was sleep. . . .

But someone was fumbling with the waistband of her jeans. She muttered petulantly, 'Go away! I'm tired.'

There was a thread of laughter in Ross's voice. 'You can't go to sleep in those clothes, Sharon. Where's your nightdress?'

Her eyes flew open. 'Ross! What are you doing in here?'

The laughter was open now. 'I'm trying to get you ready for bed. Where's your nightdress?'

She struggled up on one elbow. 'I can manage.' The only illumination in the room was a diffuse glow through the drapes from the outdoor light, but it was enough for her to distinguish his strongly carved features, softened by humour, very close. Feeling oddly breathless, she said at random, 'Whatever will Jock think? Of you being in here, I mean.'

'He's gone to bed himself. Lift up your arms, Sharon.'

She should tell him to leave, she thought in confusion. She really should. But she didn't want to ... his presence in her bedroom, the unforced intimacy of his words, his gentleness to her after the harsh words they had exchanged earlier in the day, all combined to make her want him here. And besides, deep within her, there was a treacherous stirring of excitement, the spark of fire he could kindle within her so easily. . . . Slowly she lifted her arms, wincing a little as a shaft of pain shot through her shoulder muscles.

'Sore?'

'Mmm. . . .' He was pulling her shirt over her head and she shook her hair out, stretching her neck in unconscious provocation, almost prepared for his next words.

'You're so beautiful, Sharon.' He leaned forward and she waited for his kiss, knowing how much she wanted it. Then he stopped suddenly, his voice sharp. 'What happened there?'

Puzzled, she followed the direction of his gaze; along the line of her collarbone was an oval bruise, purple against her skin, a matching one on the other collarbone. 'I expect it's where you were holding on to me earlier, while you were telling me about Peter,' she said matter-of-factly. 'I bruise easily—don't worry about it.'

'God, Sharon, I didn't mean to hurt you!' He bent his head, laying his lips on the bruise as gently as he could, as if his touch could heal what he himself had inflicted.

Her arms curved around his body, holding him there. She rested her cheek on his hair; it was thick and soft, a sprig of hay tickling her nose. She closed her eyes, the better to savour the weight and warmth of him, and the paradoxical blend of peace and excitement that seemed to be possessing her. The tide had turned again, she thought; Ross was as close to her now as he had been far away this afternoon.

Very slowly he raised his head, his eyes on a level with hers. 'I like feeling your arms around me,' he said softly. 'I think you've cast a spell over me, Sharon, with your long black hair like the wing of a raven, and your eyes the colour of the wild violets that grow by the brook in the spring.' With his finger he traced the line of her cheek to the corner of her mouth, gently teasing her lips open; they quivered at his touch until he stilled them with his own. It was a kiss that seemed to go on for ever, a kiss in which she was drowning, laved in warmth and a happiness illusive as quicksilver.

When his mouth finally left hers, she was aware of a sense of loss, acute and physical. She looked at him with eyes from which pleasure faded, to be replaced by bewilderment. 'I must be bewitched too,' she murmured huskily. 'I've never felt like this before . . . why should that be?'

'Perhaps it's a gift we shouldn't question.' Lightly he touched the smooth skin under her eyes, smudged with the same violet as her irises. 'You look worn out—you must get some sleep.'

As he drew back a little, she had to quell the urge to pull him close again, to tell him to stay . . . wanton thoughts that brought a tinge of colour to her cheeks. 'All right,' she said submissively, her lashes falling to hide her eyes.

It was as if he had read her mind. 'I don't want to go, Sharon—I want to stay. Here with you, in your bed.'

His lips brushed hers. 'But I have enough sense left to know that wouldn't do.'

This time when he pulled back she let her arms drop to her sides, her shoulders drooping a little. She wanted to ask why it wouldn't do; instead she said, with commendable casualness, 'Goodnight, Ross. I'll see you in the morning.'

He turned away abruptly and left the room, closing the door quietly behind him. Sharon sat where she was, immobile, staring at the closed door as if it could answer the questions teeming through her brain. What happened to her when Ross came near her? Why did she respond to him so brazenly? Why was it he who had awakened bodily needs and sensations that had laid dormant since she had first turned the page from adolescence to womanhood?

Unanswerable questions. Frightening questions, for by his mere physical presence he made her aware of her own vulnerability.... She stood up, dropping her clothes in a heap on the floor, pulled her nightdress over her head, and fell into bed. Sleep washed over her in a black tide, smothering her in its depths.

Sharon awoke with a jerk, some sixth sense telling her instantly that she was late. Five past seven, the little bedside clock said. Oh no, she had forgotten to set the alarm! Why hadn't Ross woken her?

Dragging on the same clothes she had worn yesterday, she stumbled into the kitchen. Empty. The coffee pot was simmering on the back burner, but she manfully ignored it, going to the back door and thrusting her feet into her rubber boots. Ross was the only person in the barn; he was three-quarters of the way through the milking. Grabbing her stool and dunking the nozzles in the disinfectant, she sat down by the next cow in line. 'Why didn't you wake me?' she demanded fuzzily.

He grinned across the aisle at her. 'You looked so peaceful, lying there fast asleep—I didn't have the heart.'

'You mean—you were in my room?' Hurriedly she

attached the milker so she would not have to look at him.

'It's becoming a habit, isn't it?'

There was something in his voice which made her look up despite herself, and at the expression in his eyes she felt herself blush, a very comprehensive blush that she was powerless to prevent. Having had no sisters or brothers, she was not used to being teased, and could think of no quick, casual quip with which to reply; matters were not helped when Ross added kindly, 'You do realise that's Melanie you're milking? Don't get kicked again. Although the bruise you got yesterday is a most interesting colour—purple like your eyes.'

'That wasn't how you described the colour of my eyes last night,' she retorted incautiously.

He laughed. 'It wasn't, was it?' he agreed cheerfully, adding with a totally unromantic pragmatism, 'Do you know that Myrtle gave forty-eight pounds yesterday? She's finally mending her ways.'

Subduing a childish urge to pull a rude face at him, she responded sweetly, 'It's because I did the milking yesterday,' and bent her head to her task again. Exasperating man! Infuriating and unpredictable man! Yet—and she paused in her task, her brow furrowed thoughtfully—how much more interesting he was, how much more fun, than Roger, whose smooth charm and urbane, sophisticated manner had formerly so impressed her. Roger would have considered it beneath his dignity to have teased her.

'Have you finished with that?' Ross asked with exaggerated politeness.

She blushed again, realising she was standing thunderstruck in the middle of the cement walk clutching the pail of disinfectant. 'Yes,' she muttered crossly, and this time began concentrating on what she was doing, refusing to think of either Ross or Roger.

They were soon finished and walked up to the house together. It was raining steadily, the faraway promontory shrouded in mist. As Ross held open the porch door for her, he said casually, 'Didn't you mention when you first came here that you had a relative nearby? Today would be the day to visit her—we certainly can't do any haying.'

It stopped her dead in her tracks. She blurted, 'How can I go and visit her—I don't have a car.'

'No problem. You can take mine.'

She shook her head. 'I wouldn't want to do that.'

'Why ever not?'

Sharon crossed the kitchen quickly, got out a mug, and poured herself some coffee. 'I just wouldn't, that's all. Do you want half a grapefruit?'

'No, thanks. Why don't you want to go and visit your relative, Sharon?'

'You've got it all wrong,' she said with complete untruth, glaring at him across the table. 'I've never liked driving anyone else's car, that's all.'

'Then it's time you changed,' he said inflexibly. 'You'll take my car and you'll disappear for the rest of the day—do you realise you haven't had any time off since you came?'

'I'm not complaining, am I?'

As if she hadn't spoken, he added, 'I really don't care what you do or where you go—just as long as you aren't underfoot here.'

'So now you're trying to get rid of me!' she snapped, the coffee and the grapefruit completely forgotten in this new clash of wills.

'Only for a few hours.' Although he was smiling, his eyes were watchful. 'We don't have to milk until five.'

In reminding her of her grandmother, he had thrust upon her a decision for which she was not ready. She said sharply, 'I fail to understand you, Ross Bowen. You think I'm capable of stealing drugs and selling them to the highest bidder, yet you'd hand over your car without a moment's thought. Hasn't it occurred to you that I might steal that as well?'

His answer was to push back from the table, get a set of keys from the ledge over the sink, and toss them down in front her. 'The car's in the shed by the gate. The tank's full of gas. Drive carefully.'

'And if I don't get home on time, how soon will you call the police to report a theft?' she demanded, horrified by the shrewish note in her voice but unable to stop herself. 'Five after five?'

'Oh, I might manage to wait until five-thirty. Don't be a bitch, Sharon—it doesn't suit you.'

She picked up the keys and shoved back her chair, her appetite gone. 'Thank you,' she said with patent insincerity. 'Let's hope you don't regret your generosity.'

Ross's eyes were the opaque blue of ice. 'I'm sure I won't,' was all he said, but at the implicit threat in his words, she suddenly shivered.

With ignoble haste she left the room, hurrying to her own room and banging the door shut behind her, throwing the keys on the crumpled bedspread. *Now* what was she going to do?

As if impelled by a force stronger than herself, she went to the closet, reached into the front compartment of her backpack and pulled out the letter that was hidden there. A letter written by her grandmother to her mother twenty-five years ago. The grandmother she had not even known existed until last January. . . .

After the death of her parents, it had been left to Sharon to sell the furnishings in the house, keeping only a few books and a couple of pictures for herself, and to go through all their personal effects. In one of her mother's drawers she had found a bundle of snapshots and letters. The photos included one of herself, taken as a very small child, sitting on her mother's knee; but most of them were of Graeme and Elizabeth Reid, presumably around the time of their marriage: her tall, handsome father with his romantic dark eyes and the lock of hair falling casually across his forehead; her beautiful, wilfull mother, chin raised, eyes challenging the future. In every photograph they were touching each other, a pattern with which their daughter was very familiar: there had always been an intimacy between her parents that had excluded her from the day she was born.

Along with the photos there had been three letters, all written in the same elegantly sloping handwriting. Aware that she could well be trespassing on territory

that did not concern her, Sharon had read them, and
then read them again, in growing consternation. They
were all from the same woman, Rowena Nichols by
name, who was her mother's mother, and who lived in
Nova Scotia. She, Sharon, had a grandmother, of
whose existence she had been kept in ignorance ... she
had read the letters once more, more discerningly this
time, and through the closely written pages had gained
a picture of a proud, reticent woman put in the position
of being forced to beg. It became obvious that Elizabeth
had married Graeme against her mother's wishes, and
had fled to Montreal with him, cutting all the ties with
her old home and her mother. Three times Rowena
Nichols had written. And from the tenor of the last
letter, Sharon could tell that Elizabeth had never
replied. . . .

It was a discovery that had rocked Sharon's world.
The death of her parents had left her, so she had
thought, totally alone, without kin. Now, if Rowena
Nichols was still alive, she had a grandmother, a blood
relation. Immediately she had resolved to get in touch
with her in the hope that the old rift could be bridged.
But the theft of drugs had occurred only two days later,
while she was still struggling with the composition of
her letter to Rowena; and the nightmare weeks that had
followed had driven all thoughts of contacting her
grandmother from her mind. But then, after the inquiry
and after she had stayed at the hospital long enough to
prove to herself and to everyone else that she was not
running away, she had conceived the idea of travelling
to Nova Scotia to find her grandmother, of simply
arriving on the doorstep unannounced. Elizabeth's
daughter, finally come home. . . .

It had seemed a fine idea in Montreal. Now, as
Sharon gazed at the letter in her hand, which she could
have quoted from beginning to end, it seemed a
terrifying prospect. To start with, Rowena might well
be dead, which would mean that the old family quarrel
would never be mended and that Sharon was indeed
alone in the world. If alive, her grandmother must be an
elderly lady who would perhaps not welcome any

revival of old, bitter memories ... yet if she, Sharon, pursued the matter no further, she would never know the truth, and would be haunted by regrets for the rest of her life.

She got up, carefully tucking the letter in her slim leather pocketbook, and going into the bathroom to shower and wash her hair. When she came back into the bedroom and took from her closet the only dress she had brought with her, she knew the decision was made. She took her time getting ready, arranging her hair in a loose knot on the top of her head with strands curling around her ears, and applying soft mauve eyeshadow to her lids and mascara to her lashes. Her dress was of a mauve knit fabric edged with white, severely styled with a V-neckline, short cap sleeves and a straight skirt slit above the knee, and gathered at the waist with a plain white belt. It suited her slim figure to perfection, her high-heeled white sandals further emphasising the slender length of her legs.

When she went out into the kitchen, Jock was alone there. His shrewd grey eyes looked her up and down in frank approval. 'Very nice, miss,' he said. 'First time I've seen you in a dress. Worth waiting for, if you don't mind me saying so.'

Sharon grinned at him as she poured herself a cup of coffee and buttered a scone. 'Not at all. Jock, can you give me directions to Riverford?' Listening carefully, she jotted down his instructions on the back of Rowena's envelope, finished her coffee, and stood up. 'Tell Ross I'll be back by four-thirty. See you later.'

She went out into the back porch to get her poncho, which unfortunately was the only rain garment she had. It didn't exactly go with her dress, she thought, surveying it ruefully, but it would have to do. Then the door opened behind her, and turning around, she saw it was Ross.

He stopped dead, halfway in the door, his eyes trained on the girl's slim figure in the mauve dress. 'Sharon,' he said, in a voice she had never heard before. Moving like a man in a dream, he pulled the door shut and stepped closer to her, shrugging off his wet rain slicker as he did so.

She waited, feeling her heartbeat quicken in her breast at the intensity of his blue eyes. 'I—I'm just about ready to go,' she said weakly.

It was as if the communication between them was on two levels, for while he was saying quite prosaically, 'I'll loan you an umbrella—it's warm enough that you don't need a coat,' his eyes were giving her another message, that he found her beautiful and desirable, that he wanted to hold her in his arms and kiss her into submission.

She could feel the colour creeping into her cheeks, but bravely she held his gaze, refusing to let her eyes drop. Continuing the charade, she said with assumed calmness, 'Thank you—I'd appreciate that.'

'I'll be right back.' He brushed past her, returning in a few moments with a silver-handled black umbrella. When she reached out to take it, his hand remained wrapped around hers. 'You look very lovely,' he said softly, his gaze wandering over her flushed cheeks and wide-held eyes, over the crown of shining black hair that seemed too heavy for her long, slender neck. 'You're a mystery to me, Sharon. I want to trust you, you know how much I want to trust you. But it's as if at the last moment something comes between us. An image of Peter's face the last time I saw him—that's what it is. And that's what stops me every time.'

Sensing that he was speaking as much in an effort to understand himself as to communicate something to her, she said gently, 'I can understand that—his death was a terrible tragedy. And there's nothing I can do to convince you of my innocence. I can only reiterate that I didn't do it.' She smiled wryly. 'Which isn't much help, is it?'

His face strained, he repeated as if by rote, but, she couldn't help noticing, without much conviction, 'You didn't do it.' In a gesture of sudden violence, he drove his fist against the doorpost. 'It's no good, Sharon.' He turned away, his voice flat. 'You'd better go. Have a nice day, and drive carefully.'

Tears stung at her eyes as he walked away from her into the kitchen, and fiercely she blinked them back.

Why should it matter what he thought? Why should she care? He was merely her employer, and a temporary one at that.

She let herself out of the house and made a dash for the car, which someone, presumably Ross, had parked near the house. It wasn't until she was sitting in the bucketed leather seat gazing at the padded dashboard that she realised this was no ordinary car; opening the glove compartment, she found the owner's manual, and discovered to her consternation that she had the use of a sports model Mercedes. Blushing a little as she remembered her provocative remarks to Ross about car theft, she turned the key in the ignition and carefully studied the controls before easing the car into first gear.

For the first fifteen or twenty minutes, Sharon's attention was occupied by the car; it was a superb piece of machinery, responding with smoothness and efficiency to her somewhat tentative handling. Then as she gained confidence she was able to spend more time appreciating the scenery. She did not plan to arrive at her grandmother's until after lunch, so she spent a leisurely morning doing a little shopping and sightseeing, before driving the last twenty miles or so further west to Riverford, which turned out to be a small town with elm-lined streets midway between the North and South Mountains. She pulled up at a garage, leaning out of the window and saying to the overalled attendant, 'Could you tell me where a Mrs Rowena Nichols lives, please?' Not until she actually phrased the question did she realise how much depended on the reply; she waited, her heart in her mouth.

'Old Mrs Nichols?' He pointed a grease-stained finger down the road. 'Go half a mile or so, turn left by the church and go another—oh, say three-quarters of a mile. There's an iron gate with the name Meadowbank on it. That's her place.'

The name was familiar from her grandmother's letters. Sharon gave the man a dazzling smile and pulled back on the street. Within ten minutes she had arrived at the gate he had described; it was open, flanked by rigidly trimmed privet hedges which looked rather incongruous against the backdrop of hardwood and fir trees. She turned into the gravelled driveway, hearing her heartbeat echo in her ears as she wound through the trees, the lane finally emerging into a sweep of manicured green lawn dotted with a harmonious arrangement of shade trees and shrubs. The house was, to her twentieth-century eyes, something of a monstrosity, combining as it did rather too many Victorian excrescences with vast quantities of brick and tile and leaded glass; but it was solidly built, beautifully kept up, and unquestionably the house of a woman of means. She parked the car in front of the veranda, walked up the stone steps between the gloomy banks of yews and rhododendrons, and pressed the bell. It somehow came as no surprise that a uniformed maid opened the door.

'Good afternoon,' Sharon said with the clarity of extreme nervousness. 'Is Mrs Nichols home, please?'

The maid was younger than Sharon, and in something of a similar state of nervousness. New at the job, Sharon wondered, or was her grandmother a martinet? 'Whom shall I say is calling, please?' the maid asked, repeating a phrase that was plainly much-rehearsed.

Sharon swallowed. 'Sharon Reid, from Montreal,' she said baldly.

'Come in, please. One moment while I check with Mrs Nichols.'

It was several minutes before she reappeared, however, a lapse which gave Sharon time to examine every detail of the gleaming oak panelling, polished brass wall sconces, and exquisite antique carpeting in the entrance hall. She could not help comparing this opulence with the threadbare furnishings of her old house in Montreal, and more and more found herself wondering about that quarrel of twenty-five years ago; if Elizabeth Reid had turned her back on maternal authority, she had also turned it on considerable wealth.

'Mrs Nichols will see you now.'

Sharon jumped. 'Oh, thank you,' she murmured, following the maid along a long, dark passageway to a sitting room at the back of the house, where the rain-spattered, mullioned windows overlooked rolling fields and the meandering course of a river, its banks shaded by elms and willows. She gained a confused impression of ornate mahogany furniture, depressingly dark oil paintings, and mind-boggling quantities of bric-à-brac, before her attention focussed on the slim, white-haired figure sitting bolt upright in a wooden-backed chair designed for fostering a correctly Victorian attitude of rectitude rather than adding to the sitter's comfort. A pair of faded violet eyes scrutinised Sharon minutely, from head to foot without registering either approval or disapproval. 'You gave your name as Sharon Reid,' Rowena Nichols said coldly. 'Am I to understand you are Elizabeth and Graeme's daughter?'

As she had not been invited to sit down, Sharon remained standing. Her mouth dry, she managed to say with a degree of composure, 'Yes, I am.'

'My lawyer was kind enough to inform me of their demise,' Mrs Nichols said with a noticeable lack of emotion. 'He also informed me of your existence, a fact of which I was ignorant. Why have you come here?'

All her sympathies with her mother, Sharon replied, 'Until a short while ago I didn't know of your existence, either. It wasn't until I went through my mother's papers that I found three letters from you. I decided, rather than writing to you, to come and see you in person.'

'How very precipitate—all the way from Montreal!'

Sharon flushed at the barely veiled sarcasm. 'Yes.'

The violet eyes never blinked. 'So your mother did not see fit to tell you you had a grandmother—I'm not surprised. She was always a strong-willed and obstinate girl.' Without any change of inflection she said, 'When did you discover the letters?'

Impossible to lie to a direct question. 'In February.'

'It is now June. Did it take you that long to find out I am an extremely wealthy woman?'

Sharon's jaw dropped inelegantly. Then she snapped it shut, losing her temper in a glorious rush of adrenalin. 'I have no idea of your financial status, Mrs

Nichols,' she seethed, her purple eyes vivid with anger. 'Nor am I interested in it. I *had* hoped we might be friends—we are, after all, members of the same family, the only members left—but I see that's impossible. Please don't get up—I'll see myself out.'

She turned on her heel and was halfway to the door when Rowena Nichols spoke, a very different note in her voice. 'I owe you an apology, Sharon. Please forgive my rudeness.' Sharon's footsteps slowed. Almost unwillingly she turned her head. 'I am a very wealthy old lady who gets used to being importuned rather more than I like. I am also a crotchety old lady who spends too much time alone.'

'Now you're playing on my sympathies.'

'Shamelessly!' For the first time Rowena Nichols smiled; she looked so uncannily like Sharon's mother at her most wilful that Sharon blinked. 'Now come and sit down, Sharon, and I'll ring for tea, and you can tell me about yourself.'

Sharon did as she was bid, wincing a little as the bulbous carved flowers on the chair dug into her back. 'I shouldn't have lost my temper,' she said. 'So I must apologise as well.'

'Nonsense! I think the better of you for doing it. How old are you, Sharon?'

The violet eyes were now warm with a charm Sharon could not have resisted had she tried. She began answering the shrewdly put questions, giving a far more complete picture of the difficulties of her home life than she realised. 'So you were always short of money,' Rowena mused. 'How like Elizabeth to cut off her nose to spite her face! She knew she had only to ask me ... but I suppose she never forgave me for calling Graeme Reid one of the most obscure of our minor poets.'

'I don't imagine she ever did,' Sharon said evenly.

Rowena sighed. 'I *was* too hard on her, I see that now. But I felt she was throwing herself away.'

'She always loved my father, and devoted her whole life to him.' Sharon's voice was gentle, for she could see the two sides of the picture and could sympathise with both Rowena and Elizabeth. 'But it's a pity she never answered your letters. And even more of a pity she never told me about you.'

'Well, you know about me now,' Rowena rejoined with a touch of the tartness Sharon already knew was characteristic. 'Tell me why you left Montreal.'

Somehow, she could not have said why, Sharon found herself pouring out the story of the drug theft and the inquiry, and her resignation from the hospital three months later. She finally stumbled to a halt. Rowena said matter-of-factly, 'As you obviously didn't do it, do you have any idea who did?'

Sharon stared at her. 'Everyone at the hospital, except for my friend Joan, thought I did it.'

'I'm not everyone, my dear.'

Blinking back tears, the girl confessed, 'I did wonder about one of the night nurses. But I had not one iota of proof.'

'A pity. What's this Ross Bowen like?'

Tricked into honesty by Rowena's rapid change of subject, Sharon blurted, '*I* don't know! Sometimes I like him so much, and other times . . . he thinks I did it.'

Rowena sniffed, an aristocratic little sniff that said volumes, and quickly Sharon spoke up in Ross's defence, telling the story of Peter's tragic death. Rowena listened impassively. 'That's some excuse, I suppose,' she admitted. 'Are you in love with him?'

Sharon flushed scarlet. 'No! Of course not.'

'I only wondered,' Rowena said mildly. 'Now, why don't I ring for that cup of tea—you'll have to be leaving shortly if you're to get back on time.'

They talked of more general matters as they sipped tea with lemon juice and ate tiny, exquisitely flavoured petits fours. Finally Sharon stood up. 'I do have to go,' she said with genuine regret. 'But I'm so pleased to have met you. It's nice to know I have a real grandmother.' Impulsively she bent and kissed the withered cheek that smelled sweetly of lavender.

'And I a granddaughter. I shall telephone you in a day or two and we'll arrange another meeting. Goodbye, my dear.'

Sharon let herself out, running down the steps and

getting back into the car. The rain had stopped, although clouds still hung low in the sky. The drive home seemed to take no time; she was singing to herself as she went, feeling miraculously lighthearted. Her grandmother believed in her, and surely in time Ross would do the same. Recklessly she acknowledged that it only needed that to make her happiness complete.

CHAPTER SIX

SHARON was about ten miles from home, driving at a leisurely pace along the winding dirt roads, when she saw a dark blue sports car stopped on the verge, the hood raised, the driver bent over the engine. There were no houses in sight, certainly no telephones. She pulled up ahead of it, leaving the Mercedes in neutral with the handbrake on, and got out. 'Can I help?' she called.

The other driver straightened and turned to face her, wiping his hands on a piece of rag. 'Why, Sharon,' he said smoothly, 'what a pleasant coincidence.'

'Hello, Greg,' she replied expressionlessly. 'Trouble?'

'I think it's either the alternator or the voltage regulator—the whole electrical system's as dead as a doornail. You wouldn't mind giving me a ride, would you?'

She did mind. But common decency forbade her from saying so. She said stiffly, 'I'm going straight to Marshwinds. Could we leave now, because I don't want to be late.'

He slammed down the hood of his car, threw the rag on the seat, and locked the door. Then he walked to the driver's side of the car, as if to open the door for her. But before she could guess his intention, he had lowered himself into the driver's seat, looking at the various dials on the dashboard with rather overdone admiration. 'So brother Ross lends you his car, does he? I have to admit he's never offered it to me—but then I don't quite have your obvious charms, do I?'

Furious for allowing herself to be so easily outwitted, Sharon said tautly, 'Greg, I'd prefer to drive. Slide over, would you, please?'

'I'm sure he wouldn't mind me driving you home.'

He grinned up at her, and she caught that faint, tantalising resemblance to Ross: a resemblance that was nothing but a mirage, she knew, for Ross was honest where Greg was devious; Ross had depths of emotion and sensitivity that Greg could never hope to achieve. If only she hadn't got out of the car in the first place. . . . 'Greg, move over.'

'No.' The gloves were off. 'You can get in the other side or you can stay here. Your choice, my dear.'

She was under no illusions about him—he would leave her here as easily as not. She stalked around the back of the Mercedes and got in the passenger side. She had barely closed the door when in a spurt of gravel and mud Greg pivoted the car in a tight semi-circle so they were facing the way she had come. The opposite way to Marshwinds . . . with terrifying rapidity, the Mercedes gained momentum, until the ditches and hedgerows were flashing past. Sharon gripped the edges of the leatherbound seat. She should have been frightened; instead she was angrier than she had ever been in her life. Above the roar of the motor and the rattle of loose stones she yelled with unladylike ferocity, 'Are you *mad*? Where the devil do you think you're taking me?'

'I thought we might go to Halifax, see a few bright lights. It's a shame to waste that pretty dress.'

'Greg Bowen, take me home this minute!'

'So it's home to you now, is it?' he said lazily, his thick hands relaxed on the wheel. 'How interesting.'

Knocked off balance, as he had intended she should be, Sharon stared straight ahead of her. Marshwinds *was* home, home as the house in Montreal had never been. As if it had been waiting for just this moment, her brain supplied the trite little phrase: home is where the heart is. No, she thought in bewilderment. She didn't love Ross. How could she? She would never fall in love with a man who did not even trust her . . . as clearly as if he was in front of her, she could see his deep blue eyes, now flashing with rage, now brilliant with desire. Love him? Impossible. . . .

It was Greg who brought her rudely back to the present. 'Ross no doubt will be somewhat displeased when you don't get home,' he gave the last word a slight extra emphasis, 'until eight or nine o'clock, won't he?'

'Things have changed since the last time you tried to make trouble between us—he'll believe me now, Greg, not you.' It was a valiant lie, delivered with just the right lack of emphasis, and with fierce pleasure she saw that Greg was disconcerted. 'So you might as well take me back now, and save yourself a drive to Halifax.'

Her voice was casual, her body in the car seat apparently relaxed. But briefly his eyes dropped to her lap where her hands rested, knuckles white with strain. 'I think not. I rather enjoy driving, particularly when it's my brother's car and I'm with my brother's—what would be the appropriate word, Sharon? Girl-friend? Mistress?'

'Try friend,' she retorted. 'You really hate him, don't you, Greg? And don't bother denying it—I know about your plan to sell Marshwinds, and I think it's the most despicable thing I've ever heard of!'

'How very naïve of you—it's nothing but a business deal. By the terms of my father's will, Marshwinds has to be sold by the end of August, and if Ross can't come up with the money, someone else will.'

Abruptly she decided to try another tack. Trying to inject genuine curiosity in her voice and yet sound suitably humble at the same time, she said, 'I don't really understand the ins and outs of it. Are you a lawyer, Greg, or an accountant? And are you based in Halifax?'

'The firm I'm with is based in Halifax, yes. Broadstairs, Hart and Bowen. Perhaps you've heard of it?'

'Well, no. But remember I'm still very new to the area.'

'I'm going to take it over in the next few years,' said

Greg, a bite to his voice that told her he meant exactly what he was saying. 'The senior man's nearly due to retire.'

As he kept on talking, Sharon listened with every appearance of interest, asking just the right questions to draw him out, subtly flattering him by her attention. Ross, she was sure, would have seen right through her act and would have given her one of those sardonic, sideways glances that she knew so well. Greg, however, could not resist the opportunity to talk about himself in front of a captive female audience, and she learned a great deal more than she wanted to about some of his business ventures. Although the picture that emerged was of a wealthy man who enjoyed power and manipulation, and who was ruthless and unimaginative enough not to care how he exercised that power, she was careful not to let him see her distaste. Eventually she steered the conversation around to real estate sales, making admiring noises as he described a couple of successful deals he had pulled off with a Montreal conglomerate firm, and venturing timidly, 'Well, as far as the sale of Marshwinds is concerned, you don't need the money, do you, Greg?' She raised large velvet eyes to his face. 'You're obviously a very rich man.'

He patted her knee, his hand resting on her leg rather longer than necessary; it took an effort of will for her not to show how her flesh shrank from him. 'I'm comfortably off, Sharon, no question of that,' he said breezily.

'So if you were to lower the price to one Ross could afford, you wouldn't really suffer financially, would you? Or aren't you allowed to do that according to the terms of the will?'

'I can sell Marshwinds to whomever I please for as little as one dollar—that would make it legal.' He looked over at her, his eyes disconcertingly cold and shrewd, all the bonhomie vanished. 'So for a dollar, Ross could buy Marshwinds—if I'd let him.'

She smiled at him as coaxingly as she could. 'Why don't you let him, Greg? You don't want the farm yourself, your interests are obviously far more wide-ranging and sophisticated than that. Nor do you need the money. It would be rather a nice gesture, I think—it would show you're man enough to bury the old family quarrel, and magnanimous enough to give your brother a helping hand.' She lowered her lashes with a charming touch of shyness. 'I'd certainly think well of you if you were to do it.'

'You'd think well of me ... would you be prepared to be a little more specific than that, Sharon?'

She risked a quick upward glance through her lashes, made uneasy by something in his voice. 'I don't understand.'

'It's very simple.' Again his hand rested on her knee. He was wearing a diamond signet ring on his little finger: she had never liked such rings on a man. 'You're a very beautiful young woman, and I don't really see why my brother should have exclusive rights to you. Transfer your—er—affections to me, Sharon, and I'll see what I can do about the price for Marshwinds.'

'If you're insinuating I'm Ross's mistress, you couldn't be more wrong,' she said in a choked voice.

'Sure,' he replied with heavy sarcasm. 'If you're not, then he's more of a fool than I think he is. But that's beside the point. Associated with me, you could go places, Sharon. And Ross could end up with Marshwinds ... which in the long run is probably more important to him than any woman.'

She had a horrible feeling that he was right, that Ross would sacrifice anything or anyone to keep his beloved farm—including herself. Would he really care if she became Greg's mistress, as long as it meant he could keep Marshwinds? It was a question she found she did not want to answer.

As if he had read her mind, Greg sneered, 'I'm right, you know—all he really cares about is Marshwinds. I'm a much better bet, Sharon. I'll show you a good time, take you to all the right places, introduce you to the right people. We could have a lot of fun.'

For a wild moment she wondered if she could do it. Endure Greg's twisted sense of values. Put up with a physical relationship with him. And in return, know

that Marshwinds would be secured for Ross, the home
that he had never had. The place he loved.

As if he sensed her weakening, Greg slowed the
car, pulling over on to the edge of the road. Turning
off the engine, he slid an arm around her shoulders
and pulled her to face him. His kiss was without
subtlety or tenderness, or even, she sensed in some
dim recess of her mind, respect. She tried to pretend
to herself that it wasn't happening. She tried to think
of Ross and Marshwinds. But neither ploy worked.
Greg's moist mouth, the wet thrust of his lips, were
all she could think of, and with all her strength she
suddenly pushed him away, her whole body taut with
revulsion.

Although he was breathing hard, Greg's eyes were as
flat and pale as a sheet of ice. 'So that's my answer,' he
rasped. 'Ross is good enough for you, but I'm not.
We'll see if Ross is still good enough for you when he's
turned off Marshwinds! Until his inheritance comes
through in three years, he won't have a cent, you
know.'

For the second time that day Sharon lost her temper.
'I don't give a hoot if he's a pauper!' she cried. 'He's
ten times the man you'll ever be.'

Greg's mouth tightened cruelly. 'To start with, he's a
bastard—and I mean that literally.'

'I'm well aware of Ross's parentage. He told me
about it himself. At least his mother loved his father,
which is more than can be said in your case!'

There was an ugly flush on Greg's heavy features. 'So
he told you about that—how interesting! I've never
known him to talk about it to anyone before.'

'It's surely no secret,' she retorted sharply.

'As far as Ross is concerned, it is. He can be as close-
mouthed as a clam when he wants to be.'

Although she was frightened by the calculation in
Greg's eyes, her brain was busy assessing what he had
revealed. It would seem Ross had trusted her enough to
share information of a highly personal nature that
normally he kept to himself . . . why had he done that
when he could not bring himself to trust her word as far

as the theft was concerned? Like so much of his behaviour towards her, it was a mystery.

She came back to reality to find Greg making a U-turn in the road. 'We'll head back now,' he said abruptly. 'You'll be late enough to have worried him, not so late he'll have called the police. And I want you to be there when I give him the notice of sale—It should be rather enjoyable.'

She could find nothing to say in reply. Relived that he had not pressed any more of his lovemaking on her, she sat quietly as the Mercedes ate up the miles back to the farm. She had no idea what kind of a situation she was going to walk into there, although she was sure it would not be pleasant. But there was no use in worrying. There was nothing she could do to avert it. . . .

It was nearly seven when Greg swung the Mercedes between the white-painted gateposts at the farm. He drew up by the dairy barn, got out, and came round to Sharon's side of the car, taking her by the arm. Instinctively she tried to pull free, but his hand only tightened its hold around her bare flesh. 'Come on,' he said. 'I presume Ross will still be in the barn. He'll be running behind schedule as he hasn't had any help.'

'And whose fault is that?' she retorted childishly, stumbling a little in her high heels on the rough ground as they approached the big sliding doors that led to the cow stalls. The interior was cool and dark, the air filled with the rustlings of straw and the distant hum of the vacuum pump. The row of cows gazed at them incuriously, jaws moving in a steady sideways rhythm as they chewed. Then to her left there was the clatter of a milk can against the cement floor; she saw Ross's tall figure come striding towards them, and felt Greg jerk her closer to him. Off balance, she was forced to lean against him, her body a slim curve in the mauve dress. Although she pulled away as quickly as she could, she was afraid she was too late: against the light behind them, Ross would only have seen the silhouette of two bodies intimately close.

'So there you are!' Greg said cheerfully. 'My car

broke down, and Sharon was kind enough to give me a lift in yours.' He smiled down at the girl standing silently by his side, her face perfectly blank. 'We came home by rather a roundabout route—but I'm sure you don't blame me for agreeing to that, do you, Ross?'

'Sharon?' Ross said very quietly, as if Greg had not spoken.

He was wearing an open-necked shirt, sleeves rolled up as usual, his jeans tucked into steel-toed work boots. He looked large and tough and very formidable, his blue eyes carefully withholding judgment as he waited for her to speak. She took a deep breath. 'Greg took the wheel of the car after I'd got out to see if he needed help. He took me nearly to Halifax and back. That's why I'm late.' There was nothing more she could add. Helplessly she waited, already braced for disbelief, derision, scorn.

Ross came a couple of paces closer. 'Why don't you let go of her arm, Greg?' he said, so casually Sharon was almost deceived; it was not until he stepped into the daylight himself that she saw the clenched fists at his sides and the menace in the hard line of his jaw. Briefly Greg's nails dug into her flesh, twisting so that she nearly cried out in pain, before releasing her. Automatically she rubbed her arm with her other hand, her eyes glued to Ross's face. For a moment she thought he was going to strike Greg, so angry did he look, and beside her she felt rather than saw Greg brace himself for the blow. But by an intense effort of will Ross controlled himself. 'If you ever lay a finger on Sharon again, you'll never know what hit you, Greg,' he grated. 'Is that clear?'

'So you've fallen for that wide-eyed, innocent look, have you, little brother?' Greg sneered. 'You're not the only one, you do realise that, of course?'

'Shut up,' Ross said crudely. 'Cut your losses, Greg— you tried to make mischief, and it didn't work. Too bad, eh? Doug's over by the chicken barn. Ask him to tow your car into town for you. Sharon, if you could get changed,' he grinned at her so infectiously that her heart lurched in her breast, 'not that you don't look charming, of course—you could lend a hand. I had to give that new Holstein an antibiotic shot, so you could do her separately and pour the milk out.'

She felt the corners of her mouth tilt in an answering smile, her eyes vivid with a happiness she wanted him to see, for he had believed her word over Greg's. He had trusted her. 'Sure——' she began.

Then Greg's voice cut in. 'You're forgetting something, Ross. I wasn't just out for a drive in the country. And while it was very pleasant seeing Sharon again,' he flicked her a venomous sideways glance, 'that wasn't the real purpose of the visit either. I've got something for you.' From the pocket of his summerweight jacket he pulled out a long white envelope. 'I believe you asked for this.'

The notice of sale for Marshwinds, Sharon thought sickly, watching as Ross took the envelope from Greg and shoved it in his hip pocket. Greg said balefully, 'Aren't you going to open it? I think you'd better—it may not be quite what you were expecting.'

Attuned as she was to every nuance in Ross's expression, Sharon caught the quick flicker of emotion in the guarded blue eyes. But as he pulled the envelope from his pocket and slit it open with his thumbnail, he could have been opening something as inconsequential as a feed bill. His eyes ran down the single page with lightning speed.

The colour drained from his face. He crumpled the letter into a ball, the thick legal paper crackling. 'You bastard,' he whispered. 'You've changed the date to the end of July. And you've upped the price by a quarter of a million!'

'Wanted to be sure you couldn't work your way around it,' Greg said softly.

'You had no need to raise the price to do that.'

'A business associate of mine is quite interested in the place. I've shown him photos, but I'll probably bring him out in the next few days to see it. You'll have all the books available, eh, Ross?'

Greg was rubbing salt in the wound, Sharon thought wildly, and how he was enjoying it. Ross's face was ashen; she could hear his rapid, shallow breathing. Unable to bear the tension, she looked ostentatiously at her watch and said to Greg, 'Doug leaves for home very shortly. If you want to get your car towed, you'd better go.'

He did not like her interruption, she could tell. 'Very well,' he said shortly. He paused, giving her a look loaded with significance. 'Perhaps you'd walk over there with me, Sharon—there's something I want to say to you.'

Every instinct screamed at her to refuse. But it could be something to do with the sale of the farm, and how could she turn her back on the slightest possibility of rescuing Ross from his predicament? 'All right,' she said stiffly. 'I have to go and change anyway.'

'I'll be back in a few days, Ross, with the prospective buyer I have in mind,' Greg went on. 'He thought he might turn the land above the railway tracks into a subdivision—more profitable than the orchards. He'd have to tear them down, of course. Unfortunately the dyke land is zoned agricultural, although he might be able to find a way around that. He's got some friends in very influential places.'

'Get out, Greg,' said Ross, this time allowing the violence to show in his voice, a raw and primitive threat.

Hastily Greg stepped backwards. 'Don't work too hard, little brother. After all, what are you working for—the future?' He had been retreating as he spoke, so that once more he and Sharon were out in the open air. She stalked towards the other barn, avoiding the puddles and noticing with relief that Doug's truck was still parked outside; once she was sure they were out of earshot, she turned on Greg like a virago. 'I don't know what you want to say to me, but I'll tell you something—not for all the farms in the valley would I become your mistress. I loathe you—do you hear me?'

He surveyed her dispassionately, letting his eyes wander insolently over her temper-flushed cheeks and heaving bosom. 'It's a pity,' he said calmly. 'I thought you might reconsider in the light of the new deadline.

But I'll come up with something else, I expect. If you're interested in helping Ross out, just be sure you make the opportunity to speak to me next time I'm here. Maybe I'll have a different proposal for you.'

'What kind of a proposal?' she demanded.

'You'll have to wait and see, won't you?' He raised a hand in mocking salute, the light catching in the cold facets of the diamond on his finger. 'Until then, Sharon.'

Disdaining any reply, she turned on her heel and ran for the house, her mind in a turmoil, her one overriding need to get back to Ross. In her room she quickly donned a pair of jeans and a shirt, and in the back porch thrust her feet into her boots. She was breathless when she got back to the barn. Picking up her equipment, she went over to the Holstein she was supposed to milk. In her absence Ross had turned on the radio, rather loudly, certainly loudly enough to make conversation impossible. Taking the hint, she bent to her task, and because she was in a hurry and wanted to be finished, everything seemed to go wrong and consequently to take twice as long. But eventually she was finished, and carried the milk cans into the pump room, starting to fill the sink with suds. She heard the door open behind her, and looked at Ross across the width of the cement floor. His face was set, his expression withdrawn. No trespassing, she thought, knowing she had to disregard this. 'Is there nothing you can do, Ross?' she asked above the roar of the pump.

He was rolling up the plastic tubing. 'No.'

'But——'

'Look, just drop it, will you, Sharon?' he said tautly. 'Do your realise that in a month the whole farm is going to be sold out from under me? And there's not a single thing I can do about.'

She could have done something ... she thought of Greg's wet mouth on hers, and shivered. 'But you believed me about Greg, didn't you?' she heard herself say in a small voice.

For an instant he looked more like his normal self. 'Yes, I believed you.'

Valiantly she held his gaze. 'I'm glad.'

His smile was more natural this time. 'I'm like a bear with a sore paw, aren't I? Sorry.'

'I understand.'

'You do, don't you?' The warmth in his eyes made her feel oddly breathless. He hesitated, then went on, 'It's supposed to be fine tomorrow, but it'll still be too wet to mow. Why don't we take off for the day—pack a picnic lunch and get in the car and go somewhere. Maybe we both need to get away from this place for a few hours.'

'I'd love that.' A whole day spent with Ross: it sounded like heaven.

'Okay. Are you game for a hike?'

Sharon would have climbed a mountain to keep that smile on his face. 'Sure.'

'I'll take you out to Cape Split—you'll enjoy it.'

And so she did. The weather forecast proved to be accurate, the sky providing a brilliantly blue backdrop for a few ragged-edged clouds that drifted with the prevailing winds. After the milking was finished and Jock's usual hearty breakfast had been dealt with, Sharon went to her room to change. No choice but jeans, she thought rather ruefully, remembering Ross's reaction to her mauve dress; but she could wear her newest pair, that fitted her exactly where they should, with her scoop-necked white top that she had certainly never worn in the barn. She braided her hair into a single thick plait, bound with a leather thong, pleased to see how the white of her shirt complemented her tan. When she went back into the kitchen, Ross tweaked her braid playfully. 'You look about eighteen,' he drawled. Then as his eyes took in the swell of her breasts under the close-fitting shirt, and the neat waist and slim hips in the straight-legged jeans, he added, 'Well, maybe.'

She blushed entrancingly, very much aware of Jock standing at the counter with his back austerely turned to them. Ross was wearing his usual garb of jeans and work boots, but his blue checked shirt emphasised the blue of his eyes, and his sunstreaked hair was still damp from the shower, curling around his ears in a way that made her long to run her fingers through it. He looked large and solid and heart-stoppingly masculine; but how could she tell him that? So she said nothing, although perhaps the shy glow in her eyes gave its own message.

It was Jock who broke the silence. 'That should hold the pair of you,' he said gruffly, putting the last wax-papered package in the haversack beside him. 'I put a bottle of water and a dish in for the dog. Off you go now, before something goes wrong with one of the tractors or one of the cows decides to calve.'

'None of them are due, Jock,' Ross responded mildly.

'Away with you. Out of my kitchen!'

'Thanks, Jock,' Sharon said cheerily. 'I'll take good care of him for you.'

'You do that, lass.' He favoured her with one of his rare smiles. 'He's in good hands, I reckon.'

It was Ross's turn to smile. 'I couldn't agree more.'

Sharon was blushing in earnest now. 'Men!' she exclaimed. 'Come on, Ross.'

'Bossing me around already,' he said cheerfully, winking at Jock as he followed Sharon out of the kitchen. He tossed the haversack in the back of the car, whistling to Wolf to jump in. The dog turned around two or three times on the narrow seat, then sat down, bushy tail thumping. Just before starting the engine, Ross grinned over at his companion, lightly stroking her cheek. 'You're fun to be with, Sharon. Let's forget everything else and enjoy ourselves today.'

From the back Wolf breathed heavily in apparent agreement, and Sharon found herself laughing. 'I'm all for that!'

They drove for nearly an hour, climbing the slopes of North Mountain and stopping for a few minutes at the Lookoff where the whole expanse of the valley lay below them, a coloured patchwork of square fields and neatly rowed orchards, with clusters of barns and farmhouses like children's toys. The Minas Basin at full tide drowsed in the sunshine, its waters a deceptively placid sheet of blue. Then they crossed the plateau of the mountain, arriving finally at the crescent-shaped curve of Scott's Bay and following the dirt road to its end. Theirs was the only car in the parking lot. 'Good,' said Ross. 'It's a place you need to appreciate in solitude. Or,' he smiled down at Sharon, 'with someone very congenial!'

Never in all her dates with Roger had she felt such an upsurge of pure, dazzling happiness. A few simple words from Ross was all it had taken, she thought dizzily, watching the play of muscles under his shirt as he bent to get the haversack and swung it on his shoulders. Wolf cavorted around their feet, forgetting the dignity of his advancing years in the anticipation of an outing.

For the first mile or so the trail led through a fragrant-scented forest of fir and spruce, criss-crossed with tiny brooks where bog violets and wintergreen flowered; their feet often sank inches deep in the wet black mud. Climbing steadily, they went from one side to the other of the peninsula, Ross explaining as they went that they would be going to the very tip of the long cape that thrust itself into the centre of the Minas channel. The conifers thinned out and hardwood began to predominate, until they were walking under a canopy of maple and birch, the narrow path dappled with shadows. It was cool and quiet. From the trees came the thin peeping of juncos and kinglets; a brilliant yellow warbler flashed past, its feathers the colour of buttercups, while a woodpecker hammered at the trunk of a nearby dead tree. Fern fronds waved gently in the breeze that blew off the sea.

Because the path had narrowed, they walked in single file, Ross ahead of Sharon, Wolf making numerous detours to snuffle around the tree trunks and fallen stumps where brilliantly green mosses flourished in abundance and tiny lichens glowed with colour. Feeling the need to confide in Ross, and perhaps made bolder because she could not see his face, Sharon began telling him about her visit with Rowena the day before, encouraged by his genuine interest into sharing with him more details of her childhood, a childhood that had in many ways been basically as lonely as his own; he told her about his schooling, about some of the trouble

Greg had caused him even when he was a small boy, about certain of the more lighthearted escapades of his college days. Halfway out to the cape Wolf treed a porcupine; both Ross and Sharon had to scramble down the slope to admire the dog's handiwork before he would cease his frantic barking and rejoin them on the path. They saw rabbits scurrying along their runs in the undergrowth, and Ross spied an owl perched high in a maple tree, waiting for nightfall and its hours of hunting among the tall trees. Finally, after climbing a series of small rises and passing a deep gully on their right, they emerged through a grove of alders into the open meadows at the tip of the cape, with beyond them the blue sheen of the sea.

Ross had been out here before. Now as he walked at Sharon's side, as they approached the edge of the cliffs, he was watching the expression on her face as she drank in every detail of their surroundings. Far below them the turquoise waters of the channel were falling back from the wet grey rocks, pulled by the inexorable forces of the tides; beyond the tip of the cape where the last peaked rock thrust upwards, the water was churned into a white-flecked current that emitted a continuous dull roar like rapids in a river, while far out into the bay the great sweep of the current curved, pale, sharp-edged as a sickle and just as deadly. The only other sound came from the mewing and crying of the black-backed gulls that were nesting on the two vertical-cliffed islands that were only a stone's throw from where they were standing, yet because of the deep gorges that lay between them, were as inaccessible as if they had been a mile away. A crow, black as pitch beside the dazzling white plumage of the gulls, crowed in derision as it perched halfway up the cliff, where golden lichen clung to the rocks. The drop was dizzying. The wheel and swoop of the gulls as they lifted from the grassy cap of the island to soar on the wind currents was equally dizzying.

Abruptly Sharon sat down, her face rather pale, vaguely aware of Wolf snuffing in the grass, and of Ross squatting beside her. It was good to feel the solid earth beneath her, to be able to dig her fingers into the tufts of grass. There was something awesome in the sheer cliffs and the rip of the tide; beautiful they might be, innocently beautiful in the sunshine with the grey rocks shadowed and the water shining; but they were also deadly, sinister in their power and immensity.

'I'm so glad you brought me here,' she said finally, giving Ross a small, grave smile.

'It affects you as it affects me,' he said quietly. He had been unpacking the haversack, and passed her a sandwich and a plastic cup of juice. She began to eat, content to be silent, knowing intuitively that Ross was equally content. He had forgotten Marshwinds, she was sure, and she was glad he was having a reprieve, even if it would only be a temporary one.

After they had eaten, Ross lay back on the grass, pillowing his head on his jacket; his eyes closed and in a minute or two his breathing was deep and regular. Sharon watched him, her eyes wandering over the untidy thatch of hair, the thick, unexpectedly dark lashes, the sensitive line of his mouth, relaxed in sleep. There was no one else in the world she would rather be with, she thought, in one of those blinding flashes of insight that can catch one so unawares. His problems and disappointments were hers, just as his happiness could make her happy. She would be content to be at his side for the rest of her life.

But that was love, she thought dazedly. That she cared for him as much as or more than she cared for herself must mean she loved him ... she loved Ross Bowen. His head had fallen to one side as he slept, and she had to fight back the urge to stroke the line of his cheek, or to rest her palm against his chest to feel the slow rise and fall of his breathing. Somehow, in the short time she had known him, she had fallen in love with him: that was why her body ached for his touch, her mouth for his kisses. More complexly, and infinitely more out of reach, that was why her soul longed for the security of having him by her side always, just as he was there now. Not always talking to her, or touching her. Simply there.

Her gaze was pulled back to the angry white waters, being sucked out to sea by forces that were invisible, beyond human control. She was in the grip of such a force, she knew, and it could be as beautiful, certainly, but as deadly, too. For Ross had given no sign that he loved her. He found her attractive and desirable; he respected many of her qualities; but he did not love her. How could you love someone you did not trust? Someone who must serve always as a reminder of the tragic loss of a young life?

Her reverie was rudely interrupted by a frantic staccato of barking from somewhere to her left. Then there was a high-pitched yelp, a rattle of stones, and silence. Suddenly uneasy, she got to her feet, jogging across the grass along the edge of the cliffs. 'Wolf!' she called. 'Wolf, where are you?'

Distantly she heard a whimper, and she hesitated irresolutely. Should she go back and get Ross or should she first find out what had happened? A second whimper decided her. She skirted one deep gorge that cut into the cliff, peering queasily downwards to the rocks far below. No sign of Wolf. The whimpering was closer now, and in the next gorge that overlooked a shale beach her brief search ended. The dog had tumbled over the cliff, slid down at least twenty feet, and landed on a small, grassy ledge where he was now cowering, tail between his legs, big brown eyes fixed on Sharon in dumb appeal. Below him the beach looked a very long way down.

'Wait there, Wolf,' she called idiotically. 'I'll be right back!'

She ran back along the cliff edge, hearing Wolf's piteous cries as he felt himself abandoned by her. Ross was still asleep, his senses deadened by too many hours of work and too much worry; wishing she didn't have to wake him yet knowing she had no choice, she knelt and shook him by the shoulder.

He wakened instantly, his open eyes reflecting the blue of the sky. 'Sharon? What's wrong?'

'Wolf's fallen part way down the cliff.'

He muttered an oath under his breath. 'Darn fool

dog—chasing a rabbit, probably. I should have tied him up. Where is he?'

At the sight of Ross, Wolf's tail gave a pathetic quiver of recognition. Quickly Ross sized up the situation. 'Run back and get the haversack, Sharon, will you? There's a coil of rope in the bottom of it. I'd better stay here—if he moves at all, he could go over.'

She did as she was told. The rope was of bright yellow nylon, comfortingly strong-looking. But there was nothing in sight to anchor it to. Not a tree or a rock. Quickly, before she could lose her nerve, Sharon said, 'You'll have to lower me down to the ledge, Ross—it looks big enough to hold me. I could tie the rope around the dog then.'

He hesitated, the sun harsh on his face. 'The only other thing we can do is for one of us to go for help— we might meet someone on the trail coming out here.'

Wolf whimpered again, shifting his hindquarters, and a shower of tiny stones bounced off the rock and fell into oblivion. 'We can't do that, Ross, it would take too long—he might fall over in the meantime,' Sharon said urgently. 'Tie the rope around me and lower me down.'

'Okay—but for heaven's sake be careful!'

She stood still as Ross knotted a harness around her, and listened intently as he told her how to hitch it around the dog. Then she was sliding over the bank, very carefully looking nowhere but straight in front of her at the cliff face; she did not dare even think of what lay below. The rope bit into her flesh: she would afterwards discover it had marked her skin with ugly weals. Her fingernails gripped whatever support she could find as inch by inch she was lowered towards the ledge. To feel it, firm and solid beneath her feet, was pure relief, and for a moment she clung to the face of the cliff, weak and trembling.

'Are you okay?'

She found her voice. 'Yes.'

'Hitch the rope around the dog now—the way I showed you.'

He sounded so calm and matter-of-fact that she found herself able to do as she was told. Wolf had the sense to stand quietly as she looped the yellow rope around his chest, although he did lick her hand. Carefully she tied the knots. When she was sure he was secure, she called up, 'Ready!'

One hand locked around a protruding rock, her feet braced on the ledge, she attempted to guide the dog's agonisingly slow passage up the cliff. As tiny stones showered down on her she ducked her head, blanking out from her mind the fact that she was no longer bound to Ross by the rope. That she was held to the cliff only by her fingers. That were she to step backwards, she would step into empty space.

The wait seemed endless. Then, as if from a long way away, his voice sounding thin and disembodied, she heard Ross call down, 'I've got him, Sharon! I'm going to lower the rope to you. Tie it around yourself as I did the first time.'

Her mouth was dry, her heart pounding in her ears. Fingers frozen around the rock, clamped into place as if by a vice, she waited, her eyes glued to the rock face, every detail of the seaming in the granite engraved in her mind for ever; she was never to see that vivid orange lichen again without a reminiscent shudder. Then something brushed her shoulder, lightly, like a ghostly hand, and she quivered all over, her breath escaping from her mouth in a gasp of terror.

'Sharon—it's the rope!'

Very slowly she turned her head to see the long yellow rope hanging alongside her body. But to reach for it she would have to let go of the rocks, and she found she could not do that. Her whole body paralysed by a fear greater than any she had ever known, she stood immobile, the strand of rope that dangled not six inches from her nose as useless to her as if it were six feet away.

'Sharon, take the rope and tie it around you!'

She closed her eyes, seized by a horrifying fit of vertigo, feeling as though she was swaying backwards out over the drop. Totally disorientated, she was sure that any minute she would plummet into space, fall through the air to be impaled on the cruel rocks where the sea lapped and sucked ... then the voice spoke again, so strong and sure of itself that it seemed to pull her back, to anchor her once again on the ledge. 'Let go with your right hand, Sharon, and take hold of the rope.'

As if she was watching a movie in slow motion, she saw her hand release its hold on the rock and reach out for the rope. It felt very thin and frail, and briefly she closed her eyes again. Then once more the voice enfolded her in its strength. 'Good girl! Now comes the tricky part. You've got to let go with your other hand, Sharon, and tie the rope around your waist the way I showed you.' A pause during which she waited dumbly. 'Let go with your left hand, Sharon.'

From somewhere, she was never sure where, came an infusion of courage. She had only to obey the voice and she would be all right. Her left hand let go of the rock. Flexing her fingers, she took the rope and wound it around her waist, focussing her whole being on the task at hand. Put the rope around her body. Loop it over. Knot the end. Check that it was secure. Grip it with both hands.

'That's fine! I'm going to pull you up now, Sharon. Help me as much as you can with your hands and feet—and be careful of your face. Ready?'

She still could not find her voice. She nodded her head, not daring to look up, and felt the pressure on the rope, pulling her upwards, lifting her feet from the ledge. For a moment she resisted, mindless with panic, for the ledge beneath her feet was her only security.

'Push off with your feet, Sharon.'

The voice. She must obey the voice. She dug her toes into the cliff face to lever herself up. The rope cut into her waist and she pushed harder. Then, inch by inch, she was being raised up. She tried to guide herself with her right hand, using her feet to best advantage with every little toehold. Up and up, slowly, carefully, the steady pull on the rope from above never faltering or lessening, the voice keeping up a steady stream of encouragement. She hardly listened to the words; it was the confidence and strength she was responding to.

Finally, unbelievably, she saw in front of her eyes the grassy tussocks at the top edge of the cliff. She grabbed at them with both hands, pulling with all her strength, and saw Ross hauling on the rope, feet braced, face strained with effort, and Wolf standing at his side. She fell forward on to the grass, face buried in it, hands clamped in it, body luxuriating in it. She was safe. . . .

Ross lifted her up, his arms going hard around her, his face buried against her hair. His voice muffled now, she heard him mutter, 'Oh dear, Sharon—I was afraid you were never going to let go of those damned rocks!' His arms tightened convulsively. 'Thank heaven you're safe!'

Her fingers reached up to stroke his face, feeling the sweat that was beading his forehead. In a terrifying flashback she remembered how only minutes ago those same fingers had been fastened to the rock face and how she had been suspended in space, dizzy and frightened. She suddenly pulled away from Ross, averting her face, and stumbled across the grass away from him. Falling to her knees, she began to retch, her whole body shaken by spasms of sickness, tears pouring down her cheeks in an involuntary stream. She felt Ross grip her shoulders and gasped, 'Go away—oh please, go away!'

But he did not. He waited patiently, holding her firmly, until the spasms ceased. Then he passed her a handkerchief and said calmly, 'Wait a sec and I'll get you a drink of water.'

The water tasted wonderfully cool and refreshing. Sharon poured some on the handkerchief and wiped her face. Only then did she turn to look at Ross, her cheeks drained of colour, her lips still with a tendency to tremble. 'Sorry about that.'

He said quietly, not touching her, 'You're terrified of heights, aren't you?'

She nodded. 'Yes. I always have been.'

'I should have guessed when we first got here, and you sat down so abruptly when you saw the drop from the cliffs. Why didn't you tell me? I should never have let you go down that cliff.'

She smiled faintly. 'There wasn't any other choice, was there? I certainly couldn't have lowered you down. And Wolf might have fallen if we'd waited to get help.' Her eyes blurred with tears. Perhaps if she had not been so shaken by the events of the past hour she would never have confessed what she did, but it did not seem the time for anything less than the truth. 'All I could think of was that Wolf was Peter's dog,' she said in a low voice. 'It seemed very important to save him.'

In one swift gesture Ross pulled her to her feet and gathered her into his arms, pressing her face into his shoulder. 'Oh, Sharon,' he muttered brokenly. 'I was feeling exactly the same way. It's as though Wolf's the very last tie with Peter, and if that went, too—well, I only knew I had to save the stupid animal if it was humanly possible.' He lifted her chin so that he could look straight into her eyes, his own deeply serious. 'That was a very brave thing you did, Sharon—to go down over that cliff knowing how frightened you were of heights.'

She shivered. 'I thought I'd be able to handle it—I didn't realise I'd freeze up like that. It doesn't seem very brave to me.'

'That's true courage, to do what has to be done in full knowledge of your fear.'

The first traces of colour began to creep into her cheeks and she lowered her eyes in confusion. Loving him as she now knew she did, his words of praise touched her to the heart. She said temperately, 'Well, I'm glad he's safe.' Trying to inject a lighter note, she added, 'And you know, Ross, you have to claim a lot of the credit, because if you hadn't kept telling me what to do, I'd be down there yet.'

'Look at me,' Her eyes flew upwards in surprise. If she had been trying to make him smile she had not succeeded. He tucked a strand of hair behind her ear, as if giving himself time to choose his words. 'Rationally I can't explain what I'm about to say,' he began slowly. 'I only know it needs to be said. What you did today has proved something to me.' Absently he smoothed the line of her cheek with his finger. 'You couldn't have stolen those drugs, Sharon—I know that now. It's not in you to do something like that, you're far too brave and honest. I should have seen that sooner, but I guess Peter's death kept getting in the way. I couldn't get a true picture of you because of him.' He must have seen the sheen of tears in her eyes, because he gently rubbed her wet lashes. 'I'm sorry for the things I said to you. They were cruel, and they were untrue.'

Although the tears were sliding down her cheeks in tiny, bright droplets, her smile was lit with joy. 'I'm so glad,' she said simply. 'I was hurt that you could believe I was a thief. I'm glad you don't any more.'

Once again he held her close; against her cheek she could feel the warmth of his skin seeping through his thin shirt. She did not think she had ever been happier. Ross believed in her . . . if he could come to believe in her, perhaps equally he would come to love her, and what could be better than that?

A wet nose thrust itself between them. They separated, laughing as they saw it was Wolf, plumed tail waving, brown eyes seeming to say, 'It's my turn for some attention.'

'You're the one who started all this,' Ross scolded playfully. He hugged Sharon. 'It's rather a drastic way to find out you trust someone, Wolf, old fellow, but I can't say I'm sorry it happened now that it's over.' Wolf sat on his haunches and yawned widely, so plainly unimpressed that Ross started laughing again. He glanced at his watch. 'You know, we're going to have to head back—unfortunately the cows won't wait for us! Are you going to be all right, Sharon?'

She smiled ruefully. 'I've felt more energetic, I have to admit. But if we take our time. I'll be fine.'

Fortunately the walk back to the car was more downhill than up, and, as so often happens, seemed shorter than on the way out. When they reached the car, however, Sharon sank into her seat with a sigh of pure relief. Muscles that she hadn't known even existed were aching; she felt sore all over. As Ross reversed out of the parking lot, she closed her eyes.

The next thing she knew they were turning into the

gateway at Marshwinds, and almost immediately Ross was caught up in the business of the farm: the switch had gone on the pump in the chicken barn. She trailed into the house, Wolf hard on her heels. He flopped under the kitchen table; she headed straight for the shower, no matter if that was a foolish thing to do before going to a dairy barn and milking thirty cows. And the regular routine was picked up as if nothing had changed.

CHAPTER SEVEN

As the warm July days slipped by Sharon was to wonder sometimes if anything had changed. Out on the cape Ross had told her he believed in her, that she was honest and brave. Yet as they went about the farm, sometimes together, sometimes apart, there was no real change in his manner towards her. She knew he was preoccupied by Greg's ultimatum, knew he had spent a fruitless week going from trust companies to banks to government agencies, all without success. From a casually dropped remark of Jock's she also knew Ross was not sleeping well, although that was clearly to be read in the deeply carved lines in his face and the shadows under his eyes. It was the look of utter exhaustion on his face one hot afternoon that prompted her to say as they finished eating lunch, 'Ross, what are you doing this afternoon that can't possibly be put off until tomorrow?'

Taken by surprise, he grinned crookedly. 'Nothing, I suppose.'

'You look worn out,' she said gently.

'Yeah ... I don't know why I'm driving myself so hard. In three or four weeks it won't matter a thing will it?' He ran his fingers through his hair, adding in a rare moment of honesty, 'I guess I keep hoping that at the last moment something will turn up.'

She looked down at the table. If she had accepted

Greg's offer, she might have been able to ensure that Marshwinds went to Ross—but oh, no, how could she have done it? Remembering why she had originally spoken to Ross, she said abruptly, 'Isn't there somewhere nearby we could go for a swim? A beach?'

Again she had taken him by surprise, and she could see him assessing her suggestion. 'I know just the place—why not?' He pushed back his chair. 'Go get your swimsuit. We'll go to Whitman's Cove. We can be back by six.'

In her room she pulled on her lilac-flowered bikini under a pair of the very brief shorts and a blouse that tied under the bustline, slipping her feet into flat-heeled sandals. Ross was waiting in the kitchen in white canvas jeans and a tennis sweater, an outfit that drew attention to his rugged good looks, his head of fair hair, and his deeply tanned skin. Sharon was suddenly hit by a wave of love for him so acute that it was actually physical; as she faltered momentarily, he asked, 'Is something wrong?'

'No—no, of course not.' Her irrepressible tongue went on, 'You look very nice, that's all. I'm only used to seeing you in your barn clothes.'

'You look very nice, too—*I'm* not used to seeing quite as much of you.' His eyes glinting with mischief, he allowed them to travel down the slim length of her legs.

She blushed furiously. 'Are we taking Wolf?' she asked at random, avoiding looking at him.

'No, he hates the water. Anyway, we don't want to have to rescue him from drowning, do we?'

'One rescue attempt's enough, I think.'

'I put a couple of towels in the car—got everything you need?'

They went outside and got in the car. This time they drove towards the south shore of the province, through rolling wooded hills and scattered farms, until on the horizon they saw the distant gleam of the sea, sprinkled with small rocky islands that were covered with spruce and fir. 'The place we're going to belongs to a friend of mine, so let's hope we'll have it to ourselves,' Ross said lazily. 'I'm not one for crowded beaches and loud radios and hot-dog stands.'

Sharon laughed, and was amused all over again when they arrived at their destination, for anything farther removed from crowds and noise could hardly be imagined. They reached the cove by travelling down a narrow unmarked road, where the air was scented with resin from all the softwood trees that crowded in on the track, boughs brushing against the side of the car. The road ended in a pebbled clearing, where Ross parked the car. Below them was a three-hundred-foot expanse of pure white sand, bounded to the west and east by gaunt grey cliffs, to the south by the sparkling waters of the Atlantic. Secluded and quiet, the place was almost magical in its sense of isolation from the rest of the world.

Slowly Sharon got out of the car, her voice hushed. 'What a beautiful place, Ross!'

'I thought you'd like it.'

As if pulled by a magnet, she walked down the slope towards the sea, where white waves curled and tumbled on to the smooth sands. Like a child, she discarded her sandals partway down the beach, dropping her towel as well, and wading out into the crisp, cold foam. It broke on the rocks, sleeking the dark fronds of seaweed-like wet hair. Sharon bent down and plucked a bright orange snail from its mooring, watching it pull its foot into the shell in puny defence against the unknown marauder.

A shadow fell across her hand: Ross, standing very close to her, ankle-deep in the water. She smiled up at him completely without artifice, her face expressive only of simple pleasure in being where she was; the sea wind tossed her hair about her head and automatically she reached up to smooth it away from her face. He reached out and captured her hand in his, bringing it to his mouth and laying his lips against her palm. Her eyes widened and she stood very still, the seaweed, the snail, the waves, the beach, all forgotten: nothing left but a man's blue eyes, a man's lips warm against her flesh.

He had stripped to his swimming trunks, the sun

gleaming on the tanned breadth of his shoulders. As if she could not help herself, Sharon felt her eyes travel down the length of his body, over the tangle of golden hair on his chest, the lean hips and the long, muscular legs. He looked as she might imagine a bronzed young god would look rising from the sea, beautifully sculptured, strength and pride in every line of his body.

As if it were the only natural thing to do, she undid her blouse and took it off, and slid her shorts down, lifting each foot from the water in turn. She flung the garments high on the sand, then turned again to face Ross, her chin tilted proudly. Much as she had done with him, he conducted a leisurely and intimate exploration of her body, his gaze as palpable as an actual physical touch would have been, and when he had finished, her cheeks were warm with colour. His next actions were as inevitable as the curl and splash of the waves on the sand; he drew her to him until they were standing body to body, the tips of her breasts brushing his chest, his hands cupping her hips. His kiss was deep and hungry, her response just as primitive. Locked together, they drank of each other, and for Sharon it was both the discovery of a lifelong thirst and the assuagement of it at the same time. She clung to him, certain that she would fall if she did not; she had never known a kiss could be like this, so all-consuming and so powerful, complete and perfect in itself, yet also a beckoning, a demand for more, bringing with it an upsurge of raw desire that exhilarated her even as it shocked her by its sheer force.

When eventually Ross raised his head, she was trembling. She had felt against her the strong throbbing of his masculinity; that she was able to arouse him filled her with a wild delight, and, for the first time in her life, with the sure knowledge of her own power as a woman. In her face were wonderment and passion, clearly to be read. With a muffled exclamation, Ross rested his cheek against the smooth, shining fall of her hair, black as a raven's wing. His voice husky, he muttered, 'I have all the urges of a caveman—I want to grab you by the hair and pull you down on the sand and make love to you in the sun.' Briefly he slid his lips across the hollow of her cheekbone, and when he spoke again there was an undertone of laughter in his voice. 'But that won't do. So why don't we go for a swim instead? Nothing like the cold waters of the Atlantic for cooling one off.'

Her mouth curved into a smile. Mischief glinting in the purple depths of her eyes, she suddenly bent and scooped up a handful of water, splashing his chest and shoulders. He yelped as the icy droplets hit his skin. She twisted out of reach of his vengeful grab at her, running into the deeper water and plunging head first into the sea.

Sharon had always loved swimming for the sense of freedom and buoyancy it gave her, and she was a strong swimmer. But as her arms flashed through the sparkling water in a smooth overarm crawl, she saw Ross draw level with her, his teeth flashing white, his wet hair plastered to his scalp. She took a deep breath and dove below the surface. Opening her eyes, she saw him following her, his body wavering in the clear blue water. Her hair a fan of black about her head, her body a graceful curve, she darted towards him, boldly clasping his shoulders and kissing him full on the mouth. Then, gasping for air, she stroked upwards.

They stayed in the sea for nearly an hour, playing like a couple of children, racing and diving, hauling themselves up on the rocks to rest, plunging back into the refreshingly chill water again and again. Finally after a race which she lost by only a narrow margin Sharon gasped, 'Enough! I've had it!'

'Can't take it, eh?' Ross grinned.

She pulled a rude face, and side by side they swam back to shore. Sharon spread out her towel and flopped down on it, wringing out her hair as best she could. Then she lay back, feeling the sun strike warm on her wet body. 'Beautiful,' she murmured drowsily, the adjective encompassing the place, the sunshine, the laughter and exercise and fun she and Ross had shared.

'Beautiful, indeed.'

Alerted by something in his voice, she opened her eyes. He was hovering over her, leaning on one elbow, open possessiveness in the way his gaze lingered on her mouth and the slim line of her throat. She knew he was going to kiss her and felt her whole body come alive at the thought of it. When he bent over, her lips were soft and welcoming; pliantly she turned in his arms so they were lying side by side. For Sharon there was no holding back. With all the generosity and warmth of her nature, she responded to his every move, returning kiss for kiss, caress for caress. His hands moved from her throat, where the pulse pounded like a trip-hammer, to her shoulders, then to her breasts. When he undid the closure of her bra, the fabric fell back, and she felt first the heat of the sun on her bare flesh, then the touch of his fingers, bringing their own warmth, stroking her skin like fire. Every tiny movement burned itself into her brain. Unconsciously, driven by its own instinctive needs, her body arched itself towards him, naked flesh to naked flesh, all the hard sinewed planes of his chest imprinted on her curves and softness. He groaned her name, beginning to kiss her again, his mouth urgent on her even as his hands roamed her breasts and waist and hips, the weight of his thigh flung over her to hold her close. She was a willing captive, drowning in a great surge of longing as powerful as any tide, caught in a whirlpool of desire which drew her even deeper into its vortex. And all the time she was only too aware of Ross's pulsing response to their lovemaking, knowing deep in her heart that she could deny him nothing and that if he wished to carry to fulfilment the embrace that was consuming her, she would be powerless to resist him. More than that— would give him willingly and with love anything he asked of her.

The sun beat down on the white sand; the waves broke unceasingly on the jagged rocks; high in the air the cold-eyed gulls soared on the wind, feathers tipped with molten light. However, for the couple strained together on the beach nothing existed but themselves and the forces they had unleashed in each other. Sharon was lost to all reason and restraint, her whole being a paean of primitive love for the man at her side, the young sea god who had risen from the waves to claim her as his own. Oblivious to everything but the frenzied rhythms of her body and his undeniable response, she was all the more shocked when Ross suddenly pushed himself back from her, his hands on her shoulders holding her at arm's length, his fingers cruelly strong.

Bereft of his body heat, she shivered, her bewildered eyes searching his face for clues to this totally unexpected behaviour. His features were strained with tension; contradictorily his eyes were still blurred with desire. A double message, she thought numbly. He wants me, yet he has pushed me away. 'What's wrong?' she whispered.

'I—we've got to stop this, Sharon.'

'Why?'

The little word hung in the air between them. He was looking beyond her to the cliffs, his mouth set. 'It just can't go any farther, that's all.'

Her face scorched with shame, she said, 'I shouldn't have responded as I did—is that what you're saying?'

He dragged his eyes back to her face. 'God, no—I'd have hated it if you hadn't responded.'

'Then I don't understand what's wrong.'

His hands very gentle but equally very impersonal, he reached over and did up the top of her bikini. 'I want to make love to you, Sharon.' His smile was a wry twist of his lips. 'I don't have to tell you that, do I?' Somehow she managed an answering smile and a tiny shake of her head. 'But we can't do it. Nothing can come of it, you must see that as well as I do.'

He had picked up a handful of sand and was letting it trickle through his fingers. 'Ross, you'll think me very obtuse, but I'm still not sure what you mean,' she said evenly.

'I mean I'm in the worst possible position to be making any kind of advances to a woman. In less than a month I'll be turned off Marshwinds. No house, no land, and precious little money—anything I've made the last few years I've poured back into the place. So there you are—what kind of a prospect is that?'

Her heart was beating unevenly. 'I wasn't kissing you because I thought you were a millionaire!'

It brought him up short. His smile was more genuine

this time as he said softly, 'You're a lovely woman, Sharon Reid, did anyone ever tell you that? No matter what happens, I'm glad you came to Marshwinds. If it hadn't been for you the last little while, I'd probably have gone out of my mind. But that still doesn't alter the basic facts. The one place in the world that I care about is going to be taken from me, and I'll be left without a livelihood. So——' he tweaked her hair in an effort to relieve the strain between them, 'this is no time for us to be making love.'

Her eyes searched his face. Had he been saying that if his situation had been otherwise, he would not only be making love to her, he would be asking her to marry him? Or did he not mean that at all? It was on the tip of her tongue to say she would love him penniless or otherwise, but something held her back: an element of doubt? an innate caution about exposing her feelings and thereby making herself vulnerable? She did not know.

Briefly the sun passed behind a cloud and again she shivered. 'How's the time? Should we be going?'

He looked at his watch. 'Heavens, yes—I didn't realise it was this late.' In one lithe movement he got to his feet, reaching down a hand to pull her up. Sharon bent to brush sand from her legs, finding him watching her as she straightened. His hair had dried, curling untidily around his ears; his skin was lightly powdered with salt, as hers must also be, she supposed. For a moment she was filled with a wild longing to press her mouth to the hollow in his shoulder and lick the salt from the hard arc of bone. Afraid he would read her mind, she dropped her lashes to hide her eyes.

It was as though he had. Roughly he pulled her close, his kiss an expression of raw, unassuaged hunger. Just as roughly he pushed her away again. 'Let's go,' he said abruptly.

She trailed up the beach behind him, her feelings in a turmoil, aware of a leaden depression and tiredness settling on her with an almost physical weight. She must have been mad to have thought for one minute that Ross loved her and wanted to marry her, and was held back only by his financial status, she thought numbly. He hadn't meant that at all. Situated as he was, he was simply too proud to become involved with her in any way. Which included making love.

The other realisation that was seeping into her brain, as they got back into the car and drove away from the idyllic little beach, was that life would never again be the same for her, for with her inborn self-honesty she recognised that, had Ross not drawn back, she would have made love with him this afternoon, and that in the truest sense of the word it would have been the right thing to do. Right for her, at any rate. But right for him? How could she know that?

She leaned her head back on the seat, as the breeze stirred her damp hair, and closed her eyes in an effort to shut out the confusion in her brain. They drove home largely in silence, a silence quite different in quality from the comfortable pauses that had been between them on the way to the beach, and Sharon, for one, was glad when they turned into the gate at the farm. Bringing in the cows and milking would be a very safe and predictable occupation after all the physical and emotional conflicts of the afternoon, she thought ruefully. No surprises there.

But when they went into the kitchen, there was a totally unexpected development facing her. From his usual stance by the stove Jock said economically, 'Two letters for you, miss.'

She had tried in vain to get him to call her by her first name. 'Thanks, Jock.' She picked the letters up, recognising the handwriting on the first immediately: her friend Joan in Montreal. But the second envelope was long and official, her name and address typed, the stamped letterhead that of the hospital where she had worked. Her face paled. She stared at the letter as if it might bite her. Why should the hospital be writing to her now? She could think of no possible reason.

'Bad news, Sharon?'

She looked across the table at Ross, not even noticing Jock tactfully leaving the room. 'I don't know. It's from the hospital where I used to work.' She swallowed. 'I should open it, I suppose.' However, she made no move to do so.

'It was a bad time for you there, wasn't it?'

Her hand still rigidly clutching the envelope, she blurted, 'It was horrible! From one day to the next everything changed. The job I loved, the people I thought were my friends, the pride I took in my work—they were all taken from me. And I was left with suspicions and accusations, with people looking the other way when they saw me coming.' Her voice was shaking. 'My friend Joan—this other letter is from her—she was the only one who really stood by me. I was conscious of everyone else either holding back until they found out the results of the inquiry, or openly disbelieving me . . . it was like a nightmare from which I couldn't awaken.'

Ross said with a lightness which did not deceive her. 'Why don't you open the letter, Sharon? Maybe they're telling you they've found out who actually did it.'

'You really don't think I did it any more, do you?' Her eyes filled with quick tears.

'I'm sure you didn't.'

Childishly she scrubbed at her eyes with the back of her hand. Somehow his quietly spoken statement had given her courage to open the envelope. She pulled out the single sheet of paper and her eyes ran down the four closely typed paragraphs. The words blurred in front of her. More slowly she read them again. Her knees no longer able to hold her up, she sank down on the nearest chair.

'What is it?' Ross asked sharply.

She answered incoherently, 'There was another drug theft two weeks ago. They caught one of the night nurses—she did it. She confessed to the other theft as well. So I'm completely cleared.' Looking across at him, she added, 'They're offering me back my job as supervisor—with a pay rise.'

'Will you take it?' he rapped.

'Oh, no—of course not,' she said without even having to think of her answer. 'I'm working for you now.'

'But you won't be for much longer.'

'I don't want to leave here, Ross.'

Between them, called up by her words, yet unspoken, lay all that had happened on the beach. 'I don't want you to leave either, Sharon, but sooner or later you'll have to.'

She said stubbornly, 'We'll worry about that when the time comes.' Deliberately she picked up Joan's letter and began to read. Joan, of course, filled in all the details; her delight at Sharon's exoneration was so heartfelt that again Sharon felt like crying. It was as if an immense weight had been lifted from her shoulders; it was a weight she had learned to live with, had often not even been aware of. But now that it was gone, she could recognise what a burden it had been.

'This calls for a celebration,' Ross announced. 'We'll get the milking done, then head for Halifax—we can have a drink and a late dinner there.'

Sharon smiled with pleasure. 'I'd love to!'

'Let's get the chores done, then.'

Sharon stood up, the envelopes in her hand. Although she was not aware of it, her face was glowing with an inward happiness after having read the two letters: she had been publicly vindicated, cleared of any suspicion of a crime she had not committed. Ross said quietly, 'I'm really happy for you, Sharon.'

She looked over at him. 'You are, aren't you? That's nice,' she responded naïvely. 'You know, I sometimes think that's the mark of a true friend, someone who can genuinely share the good times. It's easy enough to find people to commiserate with you when things aren't going well. But to find someone who's made happy by your happiness—that's much more difficult.'

'I hadn't thought of it quite that way before. But I think you're right.' He leaned over and kissed her gently on the mouth. 'You're a wise and beautiful woman, Sharon.'

Absurdly she felt like crying again, tears of happiness this time. In a strange way she felt as close, if not closer, to Ross now than she had on the beach when he had been making love to her. So many ways of being intimate, she thought confusedly. A single kiss from him and she felt as though she would drown in the tide of love that had welled up within her.

'What are you thinking?'

How could she tell him? 'I—I guess I'm just glad we're friends, Ross,' she said, knowing it for the truth, even if only part of the truth.

'I'm glad we are, too. And friend's a big word in my book, Sharon—not one I take lightly.'

At the intent look in his eyes, her heart skipped a beat. It was not an avowal of love, she knew, but perhaps in its way it was almost as significant. And who knew where it might lead? Her mouth suddenly dry, she murmured, 'We'd better get on with the chores.'

'So we had.' Another of those feather-light kisses that brought a glow to her cheeks. Then he slapped her familiarly on the bottom. 'Off you go!'

She poked out her tongue, ducked his vengeful grab at her, and ran to her room to change, her heart singing. Things would work out somehow, she thought with a rush of optimism. They were bound to. . . .

That evening would long stand out in Sharon's memory as one of pure enchantment. On her shopping expedition the day she had first met Rowena she had bought a ruffled, high-waisted peasant dress, very becoming with her slenderness, while Ross looked heart-stoppingly handsome in a lightweight summer suit with a silk shirt and tie; she felt almost shy of him, so different did he seem from the man who an hour ago had been helping her haul milk cans. This immaculately dressed stranger could have held his own in any environment, she knew. Tongue-tied, she murmured, 'Are you ready?'

'It's all right, Sharon,' he drawled lazily, 'it's only me.'

She blushed. 'You have no right to look so handsome!'

Laughing, he dropped a kiss on her nose. 'Nor you so beautiful—how will I ever keep my mind on the menu?'

The restaurant was near the top of one of the tall buildings that overlooked the harbour, the city lights

spangling the darkness below, while the mooring lights
of vessels anchored out in the channel were reflected,
red, green, and yellow, in the still black waters. The
food was excellent; there was a dance floor with a small
orchestra, where they discovered they both loved to
dance; after the meal they relaxed in the bar with
liqueurs, talking over a whole range of subjects that
they continued to pursue on the drive home. Apart
from the porch light, the house was in darkness. Sharon
said at random, 'It reminds me of the first time I came
here—the house was just as dark that night.'

Ross gave an indeterminate grunt. They walked
through the kitchen and down the hall to the door of
Sharon's room, where they stopped, a constrained
silence falling over both of them. 'Thank you, Ross,'
Sharon said awkwardly. 'That was a lovely evening, I
did enjoy it.'

'My pleasure, Sharon. I—oh, hell!' His arms went
hard around her, his kiss burning against her mouth.
Her body melted into his, until nothing else existed in
the world but the fierce demand of his mouth, the
hardness of his body against hers. Her heart was racing
in her breast when he finally released her, and in the
quietness of the hall the mingled sound of their
breathing seemed to echo and re-echo. Ross's voice was
louder when he spoke. 'If things had been different——'
he broke off, staring into the darkness, his jaw a hard
line. 'But they aren't, are they? Go to bed, Sharon. I'll
see you in the morning.' One last quick squeeze of her
shoulders and he had turned away, striding down the
hall towards his own room.

Almost she called him back. If things had been
different, what then? she wanted to cry out. Are you
saying you love me? Is that what you're saying? His
door opened, then shut behind him, and her shoulders
slumped in defeat. How could she ask him such
questions? She couldn't, of course. . . .

As the next few days went by, Sharon came to the
conclusion that Ross had made some sort of decision
that night he had left her so abruptly in the hallway.

His manner towards her was courteous, even friendly at times, yet always with an undertone of remoteness, a sense of distance that she could not bring herself to bridge. It was almost as if he had relegated her to the role of employee: a valuable employee, one to be well treated, even deferred to at times, but nevertheless an employee. She noticed—for how could she help it?—that he never touched her. Certainly there were no repetitions of those devouring kisses on the beach. He had retreated to a place she could not follow, and because of the brief closeness they had shared, and his avowal of friendship, his withdrawal was all the more bitter for her. She longed for the courage to confront him, to ask him what had happened to so change him, but whenever she tried to steel herself to speak to him about it, at the last minute her heart would fail her and she would retreat to commonplace conversation or to silence.

It was in just such a silence that they were working in the barn one evening a few days later. It had been a very hot day; Sharon was feeling tired and out of sorts, her shirt sticking to her back, beads of perspiration on her forehead. Ross could have been a chance-met stranger for all the communication that was between them; Myrtle and Melanie were at their most perverse. She was crazy to stay here, she thought crossly, when she could be back at the hospital as a ward supervisor, working in air-conditioned coolness in a crisp white uniform. But even as she thought this, she knew she was fooling herself. Here, with Ross, no matter how uncommunicative he was, was where she wanted to be. Needed to be. Had to be.

Doug's dour voice broke into her reverie. 'She's in here, ma'am. Sharon—a visitor for you.'

Her hand on Myrtle's flank, Sharon stood up. 'Rowena!' she exclaimed. 'I—what a nice surprise,' she finished weakly.

Rowena stepped in the door, picking her way delicately along the concrete walkway in her pristine white shoes. Her suit was palest green. There was not a hair out of place on her head. She looked so cool and composed that Sharon felt all the more keenly her own dishevelment. She pushed a damp strand of black hair back from her forehead. 'Come and meet Ross,' she said awkwardly.

Ross finished emptying his milk can, then straightened to his full height, walking over to them. Sharon felt her heart turn over with love for him. She said, carefully ironing any emotion from her voice, 'Ross, I'd like you to meet my grandmother, Rowena Nichols. Rowena, this is Ross Bowen. My employer,' she heard herself add, then could have bitten off her tongue as Ross shot her an inimical look. Rowena and Ross shook hands, exchanging the usual commonplaces; at another time Sharon might have been amused to notice how shrewdly each was sizing up the other. Of necessity Sharon and Ross had to continue with the milking; Rowena stayed in the barn, perched incongruously on a chair Ross had produced and dusted off, asking him a series of incisive and intelligent questions that he was obviously pleased to answer. Before five minutes were up, it was plain that they liked and respected each other. Feeling rather left out, Sharon went about her work; Rowena and Ross had moved on to the current political situation, conducting a caustic assassination of the character and capabilities of one of the local politicians before moving on to the federal scene. They had dealt summarily with the Cabinet, the Prime Minister, the Opposition, and the Senate by the time the milking was done, and were clearly enjoying themselves hugely. So it came as a surprise when Ross said, 'Sharon, I'll clean up. Why don't you take your grandmother up to the house? Jock will make you both a cup of tea, I'm sure.'

'An excellent idea,' Rowena said promptly. 'Come along, Sharon.'

Annoyance struggling with amusement, Sharon meekly did as she was told. They went outside, where Sharon saw without much surprise that a black Rolls-Royce was parked near the house, a uniformed chauffeur patiently leaning on the door as he waited. Rowena said calmly, 'I drink far too much tea. Let's go for a walk instead.'

Glancing down at the white shoes which were as frivolous as any Sharon might have worn, the girl murmured, 'Are you sure?'

'I'm not in my dotage yet, child. Come along.'

Again aware of those twinges of sympathy for her mother, Sharon accompanied Rowena up the hill into the orchard. There was a light breeze blowing from the basin and gratefully she lifted her face to the cooler air, feeling some of the tiredness leave her. However, she should have known better than to relax. Rowena said serenely, 'What a wonderful view one gets from here. You do realise you're head over heels in love with the man, don't you?'

'I'm not!' Sharon sputtered, with complete untruth.

'Of course you are. My dear, if I were forty years younger I'd be in love with him myself. I suppose he's so wrapped up in the farm that he can't see you for the cows, is that the trouble?'

'He likes me,' Sharon said carefully. She met the faded violet eyes squarely. 'He's even attracted to me physically——'

'I should hope so,' Rowena sniffed. 'You're not my granddaughter for nothing. You're a very beautiful young woman and the man would have to be blind not to see that.'

'You're hopeless!' Sharon scolded, unable to prevent herself from smiling. 'But he doesn't love me, Rowena.'

'Hmm.' Her grandmother glanced out over the dykes. 'Could it be something to do with that hospital business?'

'Not at all.' Delighted to be able to share the good news she had recently received, Sharon told Rowena about the contents of the two letters she had received, and described how Ross had expressed his trust in her before the letters had arrived.

'So it's not that . . . would there be some other reason he wouldn't feel free to love you?'

There was, of course: the imminent loss of Marshwinds, and all that that entailed. As clearly as if she were back in the Victorian splendour of Rowena's house, Sharon heard her grandmother's voice saying clearly, 'I am a very wealthy woman, used to being importuned.' With those words echoing in her brain, it somehow seemed impossible to tell Rowena about Ross's financial difficulties and the stranglehold Greg had over him. 'Not that I know of,' she replied with attempted casualness.

Rowena shot her a sharp glance. 'I see. I could ask him outright, I suppose.'

'No!' Sharon exclaimed in horror. 'Don't you dare!'

'No? Perhaps you're right.' Rowena sighed. 'After all, I tried to meddle in Elizabeth's affairs and look where that got me. But I hate to see you unhappy, child.'

Impulsively Sharon gave Rowena a hug, even as a tiny part of her brain recognised that Rowena was unabashedly playing on her sympathies. 'I'll manage,' she said lightly. 'Now, how about that cup of tea?'

'Very well.' A gleam appeared in Rowena's eyes. 'I must ask your Ross——'

'He's not my Ross!'

Rowena sailed imperviously on '——what he thinks of this latest tax hike.'

As it happened, Rowena stayed for another couple of hours, the three of them sipping strawberry diaquiris in the living room; during the flow of conversation Sharon recaptured some of that earlier closeness to Ross, for he would not allow her to remain on the fringe of any of the discussions, drawing her in and by his interest causing her to expand and largely forget her selfconsciousness; although all the time she was aware of Rowena's sharp-eyed interest in what was going on.

But after Rowena had left, ceremonially ensconced in the back seat of the Rolls-Royce and waving a regal goodbye, Sharon could almost see the barriers between her and Ross fall back into place. He said, watching the car drive away, 'What a delightful woman she is—can you imagine her at twenty? I bet she led the men a merry dance!' The smile faded from his face. 'Well, I'd better go in, I have some work to do on the books. Greg's coming tomorrow.'

'With the man who might want to buy the farm?'

'Yes. His name's Keith Hastings. He's well-known—

or maybe I should say notorious—as a real estate speculator. Doesn't give a damn for land *per se*, only for what profit he can make out of it.'

'Oh, Ross. . . .' She rested a hand on his sleeve, her eyes dark with distress.

He moved away so quickly that her hand fell back to her side. 'See you tomorrow.'

She stood still in the cool night air, her nostrils filled with the sweet scent of stock from the garden, her eyes dazzled by the brilliant display of stars; but within her the pleasure of the evening died to ashes. Ross Bowen did not love her, she thought numbly; he did not love anyone. He was totally self-sufficient, cold and uncaring. The only thing he cared about was Marshwinds.

CHAPTER EIGHT

THAT this was so was reinforced for Sharon the next morning as she and Ross did the milking. He was in a foul mood, biting her head off when she dropped a milk can, the metallic clang echoing in the cobwebbed rafters of the barn. 'Can't you be more careful?' he blazed. 'I've got a whopper of a headache!'

'I'm sorry,' she said evenly; be damned if she was going to abase herself for a simple accident.

'And can't you go a little faster? I don't want to spend the whole day in here!'

This was a totally unjustified criticism, for she was proud of the steady and very efficient rhythm with which she worked. 'No, I can't,' she said shortly.

'Well, for pity's sake try!'

Dangerously near tears, she snapped, 'if you'd stop complaining, I'd get along a lot quicker.'

Ross stepped over to her, his jaw jutting out, his eyes cold and hard as ice. 'Look, Sharon, do I have to spell it out for you? This place could be sold out from under me today—what do you want me to do, dance a jig?'

'You could try acting like a decent human being instead.'

He grabbed her by the shoulders, shaking her impatiently. 'I thought you understood how I feel about Marshwinds.'

He was standing so close to her that she could see the thick fringe of his lashes. Far too long for a man, she thought irrelevantly. It wasn't fair. 'I do understand. But there are other things in this life besides a farm.'

'Not for me. Not right now.'

It was a confirmation of what she had suspected. Why then should she feel as though he had twisted a knife in her flesh? Anger welled up as a defence against pain. 'All you care about is a few acres of land and some buildings!' she stormed. 'People and their feelings are more important than any amount of property, don't you realise that?'

'Of course I do, you little idiot.' He kissed her almost as if he hated her, releasing her just as quickly and leaving her with the strange sensation that kissing her was the last thing he had planned to do. 'You don't understand at all,' he said roughly. 'I've had enough of this—let's get back to work.'

Sharon sat down by the next cow in line, a placid Guernsey named Sally, and rested her forehead on the smooth, warm flank so Ross would not see she was crying. If this was the way one felt when one fell in love, she thought drearily, why did people continue to do it? And, more than that, continue to praise the state of being in love as if it were something desirable? It was pain and confusion, that was all it was.

She purposely kept out of Ross's way for the next hour, leaving the barn by herself and going up to the house for breakfast; although he joined her there shortly afterwards, he immediately buried his nose in the latest issue of a dairyman's magazine he subscribed to, so that they ate in silence. She hurried through her meal, wanting to be anywhere else other than where she was, so close to him in a physical sense yet so far away in any other sense; she could have reached out one hand and stroked his thick, untidy hair, and so strong was the longing to do so that she actually had to clench her hands in her lap. She downed the last of her coffee in one quick gulp and pushed back her chair, saying coldly, 'I'll be in the garden if you need——'

A loud knock at the back door. Instantly she knew it was Greg, for who else would knock with that blend of force and arrogance? Nor did he wait for anyone to let him in. The door opened, there was the sound of footsteps and voices, one of them recognizable as Greg's bluff, overly hearty tones, and then two men came into the kitchen.

As always, it was Greg's intangible likeness to Ross that impressed Sharon first; it was as if a gold coin of austere and elegant design had been melted so that the outlines were blurred and distorted, and a thing of beauty had become commonplace, ugly, even corrupt.

He was walking towards her, hand held out, pale eyes full of calculation. 'Hello there, Sharon,' he said breezily.

Short of outright rudeness she had no choice but to take his hand. He pressed it meaningfully, and pulled her forward to meet his companion, a florid-faced man to whom, perhaps unjustly, Sharon took an instant dislike. 'Keith Hastings, Sharon Reid.' Greg laughed with a touch of crudeness. 'Ross's right-hand woman, Keith—lucky man, isn't he? And how are you, Ross? You know Keith, of course.'

The slowness with which Ross got to his feet was a subtle insult in itself. 'Keith and I have met, yes. It was at the hearing for the appropriation you'd hoped to pull off on South Mountain, wasn't it?'

Keith Hastings flushed darkly. 'That hearing was mismanaged from start to finish.' Deliberately he looked around him. 'Nice place, Ross. I'm looking forward to seeing it. Has a lot of possibilities.'

For a moment Sharon thought Ross was going to lose all control and strike out at Keith; instinctively she stepped into the breach, saying with a brightness that sounded totally false in her own ears, 'Can I get you a coffee, Mr Hastings?'

'I think we should get started right away,' Greg said

smoothly. 'Keith wants to get a complete picture of the place, assets and liabilities. I hope you've got the books ready for inspection, Ross?'

'As I run a straightforward and honest operation, they're always ready for inspection,' Ross countered coolly. 'I think I'll take you up on that coffee, Sharon—would you mind pouring me one?'

She would have walked across broken glass to have saved him even five minutes of what lay ahead. She gave him a smile in which, recklessly, she tried to project all her love and support, and for the first time in days saw a faint answering warmth in his face. 'You take sugar, don't you?' she said banally, the message in her deep purple eyes a very different one.

That it had been a dangerous thing to do she soon found out. Greg took her by the arm, his grip surprisingly strong for a man so obviously out of condition. 'While Keith and Ross are looking over the books, you and I have a date, I believe. You were going to show me the view from the top of the hill, weren't you?'

Her eyes flew to his face. She knew as well as he that they had no such arrangement: so he must have a new proposal for her. Or would it simply be a repeat of the first? Her flesh crawled at the thought, but at the same time she knew she had no choice but to go with him. If there was the faintest chance she could better Ross's predicament, she had to take it. She said coolly, 'So we did—shall we go now?'

He put an arm familiarly around her shoulders, half turning her so that she was facing Ross and Keith; she flinched away from the look in Ross's eyes. Although only a few minutes ago he had favoured her with one of his rare smiles, now his face was closed against her as finally as if a steel door had been slammed down. 'We won't be long,' she said helplessly, knowing with a sick feeling in her stomach that he would interpret her actions as a going over to the enemy camp—and who could blame him?

Greg's arm still lying heavily on her shoulders, they left the room together. Once outside she tried to move away. 'Let go, Greg—you accomplished what you wanted to.'

'He might be still watching. Where are we going?'

'I suppose up to the orchard,' she said with bad grace, walking as fast as she could and purposely leading him through the tallest grass she could find, hoping it would mark the light flannel of his immaculately creased trousers. Once out of sight of the house, she pulled free of him and said with calculated rudeness, 'Make it fast, Greg—and it had better be good!'

As he irritably struck away a circling insect, it was the dissimilarity between the two brothers that struck Sharon, one so completely at home in the outdoors, at one with the land he loved, the other plainly uncomfortable: behind a desk Greg would be suave and in control, whereas here he looked totally out of place.

Now that they were alone, he was no longer bothering to keep up the pretence of geniality, his pale eyes blank of expression as he looked across at her. 'I want to make a deal with you,' he said flatly. 'You made it clear last time that you won't be my mistress in actuality. What I want you to do instead is pretend to be my mistress—you and I will know the difference, but no one else will.'

'You mean Ross won't,' she said, her mouth dry.

'Right, I want you to do this for the next three weeks. In return, at the end of that time, I'll withdraw the offer to Keith and sell the place to Ross at a price he can afford.'

'How much?'

'Oh, quarter of a million, say. He could come up with that amount on the strength of the money he'll get in three years.'

'So you'll be losing half a million dollars,' she said, her brain working frantically.

He shrugged. His tailored grey suit had no doubt cost a small fortune, she found herself thinking, but not even it could disguise the essential heaviness and coarseness of his frame; she thought of the taut lines of Ross's body and was swept by a wave of physical longing for him that almost made her lose Greg's next words. 'I don't need the money,' he was saying. 'My father saw to that. Money's only good to me for the power it gives me—and it's worth any amount of money to see Ross squirm.'

'How you hate him!' she whispered.

The expressionless eyes, amoral as a cat's, ran over her face as if she had stated something so obvious as not to need saying. 'Naturally.'

'Why? What did he ever do to you?'

'You really want to know?'

She nodded.

'All right—I'll tell you. . . . I was about seven when the trouble started,' he said emotionlessly. 'Terrible arguments between my mother and my father, both of whom I adored. I felt as though the whole world was coming apart—because, of course, I had no idea what was going on. I realise now that my mother—Alicia was her name—must have met Ross's father about that time. Perhaps she was asking for a divorce, I don't know. What I do know is that she left soon afterwards. I was told the usual lies, she's gone for a visit to friends, she'll be back soon, and so on. My father wouldn't allow me to write to her or to see her; he spent a lot of time with me and through him, I grew to hate her for leaving us.'

'Where was she? Did you ever find out?'

'With her lover. Living with him quite openly and shamelessly.'

'What choice did she have, if your father wouldn't give her a divorce?'

He shot her a venomous glance. 'She should have stayed home where she belonged with her husband and her legitimate son.'

No point in arguing with him. 'So what happened?' she asked in a carefully neutral voice.

'A year later Gerald—my father—brought her back. Her lover had been killed in a plane crash, she was destitute, and she had Ross, who was only a month old. . . .' His mouth a thin line, he added roughly, 'She made no pretence of being glad to be back home with my father and me. She devoted herself to Ross. Oh, she was never cruel to me—just miles away. Unreachable. But she was different with Ross, I wasn't so young that I couldn't see that. I hated him from the moment he came in the house.'

What was there to say? A part of her could even sympathise with Greg, who, after all, had been only a small child at the time. She said carefully, 'But that's all in the past, Greg. As an adult, you must see that Ross was in no way to blame for what happened. It was between your mother and father, not between you and Ross.'

'My father never forgave Ross for even existing. Nor have I. Even my father's remarriage and Peter's birth didn't change that.' Malevolently he added, 'And now I've got the chance to get back at Ross—through the farm and through you. And I intend to take advantage of it.'

'You can certainly hurt him by selling Marshwinds, we both know that. But what makes you think he cares what I do or don't do?' Convinced of her own words, Sharon went on, 'He only cares about Marshwinds. Not about me.'

'Now that's where you're wrong. I've seen the way he looks at you when he doesn't think anyone's watching. And I saw the look on his face when I put my arm around you this morning.' He laughed, a sound devoid of humour. 'I know very well I can get at him through you.'

He was probably right. Remembering the fierce demands of Ross's lovemaking on the beach, she knew how he would hate seeing her in another man's arms, particularly when that man was Greg. It was nothing to do with love: it was simply male possessiveness. 'You say if I co-operate with you and give every appearance of being your mistress, you'll sell the farm to Ross. But what guarantee do I have of that, Greg?'

He grinned. 'You'll just have to trust me, Sharon.'

'You'd have to put it in writing.'

'Oh no, my dear. So you can run and show it to

Ross? Sorry. You'll just have to take my word for it.'

She glared at him in frustration, knowing she didn't trust him. 'I'd promise not to show it to Ross.'

'No. Nothing in writing—I'm not that gullible. And if I find out you've told Ross what's going on, the whole deal's off. Is that clear?'

It was her first real glimpse of Greg, the ruthless businessman; perhaps because she disliked him so intensely she had been in danger of underestimating him. 'I see,' she said slowly, trying to give herself time to think. 'What exactly would all this entail, Greg? What would you expect of me?'

He pulled a gold cigarette case from his pocket and lit a cigarette with a matching lighter: overt symbols of his wealth. 'We'd go out together most evenings—you're free by seven-thirty or so, aren't you? I wouldn't bring you home until late. I'd be seen kissing you, holding you—I want there to be no doubt as to the nature of the relationship. And there's another thing, Sharon.' He drew on the cigarette, lazily expelling a cloud of blue smoke that drifted across to her, unpleasantly strong. 'It would have to be convincing. No shrinking violet acts. When I kiss you, you'll look as though you're enjoying it. And you'll play up to me. If you don't then again the bargain's off. Ross is no fool. If you're not convincing, he'll figure out something's up and then it will all have been for nothing. I want him hurt, Sharon, and it will be up to you to make sure that happens.'

Her lip curled in scorn. 'You're loathsome, Greg Bowen! But I'm sure you know that.' Deliberately she turned her back on him, leaning on a branch of an apple tree, her eyes gazing unseeingly at the far horizon. She was deeply uneasy. What if she entered into this sordid bargain with Greg, which inevitably would mean Ross would end up despising her, only to have Greg renege at the last minute? It would all have been for nothing . . . but on the other hand, if she refused Greg's offer, Marshwinds would be sold to Keith Hastings and Ross would lose the only place he had ever called home.

From there it was a logical step that she should consider Ross's feelings. He wanted her, she knew that without a shadow of doubt. He liked her, respected her, and had finally come to trust her. Her mind winced away from what Greg's scheme would do to that trust. Yet he did not love her, had never said anything to her about commitment of permanence. It was Marshwinds he loved. Her true rival was all around her, green and beautiful. If only he wanted her as fiercely and possessively as he wanted Marshwinds, she thought with an ache in her heart. But he didn't, and that was that. Her sole concern must be that because of Greg's hatred, she had been given the means to enable Ross to keep his beloved farm.

She turned back to face Greg. 'I'll do it,' she said with assumed calmness, her chin tilted at an angle Ross would have recognized. 'You swear you'll keep your side of the bargain?'

'Of course I will,' he said impatiently. 'I told you, it'll be worth it for a couple of weeks—he'll think I've got the farm and his girl, and he won't like that a bit.'

Sharon hesitated, biting her lip. It was all wrong, dreadfully wrong. But surely, once it was over, and Ross had Marshwinds for himself, she could explain to him what she had done, and he would understand? Perhaps even be grateful?

'Let's go back to the house,' said Greg. 'And don't forget, Sharon—you're going to make it convincing.'

It was an hour later by the time Keith and Ross had finished the tour of the farm and returned to the house. Greg had insisted Sharon change into shorts and a top; the pair of them were sitting very close together on the chesterfield in the living room sipping sherries that Jock had somewhat grudgingly supplied. Greg's arm was lying loosely around Sharon's shoulders, his fingers rhythmically stroking her bare, tanned skin. He said bluffly, 'Well, how did you both get along? What do you think of the place, Keith?'

Ross had given Sharon one look of total incredulity, a look which struck her to the heart. Greg's fingers increased their pressure in unspoken warning, and obediently she turned her attention to him, smiling sycophantically as he and Keith exchanged a few remarks. Keith, she soon realised, was delighted with Marshwinds, sketching on a piece of paper his plans for an exclusive subdivision where the orchards now stood and talking enthusiastically about rezoning and access roads. At the first opportunity Greg said cheerfully, 'Sounds as though we may have a deal on our hands, Keith. I realise you've got a bit of research to do first, some surveying and so on, but then we can't close the deal until the end of the month anyway. Have to give Ross every chance we can, don't we?' He laughed jocularly, raising his glass in a mock salute. Then he turned his attention to Sharon. 'Looks like you might be out of a job pretty soon, sweetie. But as I told you, you don't have to worry about a thing—I'll look after you.' He squeezed her familiarly.

It was her cue. She had to say something. She smiled falsely. 'It's very kind of you, Greg,' she murmured, knowing that was the best she could do. Making a move to get up, she added, 'Why don't I get Keith a sherry?'

'Oh, Ross'll look after that, won't you, Ross? Join us, little brother, why don't you?'

'No, thank you,' Ross replied, steel in his voice. 'I'm particular about the people I drink with.'

Greg was not at all put out. 'Now, Ross, you'll hurt Sharon's feelings talking that way.'

Ross gave Sharon a cool, dispassionate glance. 'I hardly think so.'

She could feel the colour rising in her cheeks and for a wild moment was tempted to throw her glass of sherry in Greg's face and forget the whole thing. Perhaps the man sitting at her side sensed her rebellion; he nuzzled his face into her neck, choosing to ignore the rigidity of her body, and said, 'Never mind, Sharon—I don't think the woman's been born who can satisfy Ross's standards. But you and I will do just fine together, won't we?'

Again that warning pressure of his hand. She fought back a wave of sickness and smiled into his eyes with frantic gaiety. 'Sure we will—I could use a good time after being stuck out here for so long.'

'And I'll give it to you, honey,' he said meaningfully, his big hand clumsily caressing the nape of her neck.

She couldn't keep this up much longer, not with Ross standing so rigidly by the door watching Greg's every move. 'I've got to get to work, Greg,' she said lightly. 'Especially if you're going to pick me up tonight. What time did you say?'

She saw the gleam of approval in his pale eyes. 'Around eight. Wear your prettiest dress.'

'There's not much choice,' she said drily.

'I'll soon change that.' He ran his eyes over her slim figure in blatant possessiveness. 'It'll be a pleasure to buy pretty things for you. We might even squeeze in a quick trip to Montreal.' He chuckled. 'If brother Ross will give you a day off, that is—you're a real slavedriver, Ross.'

'Sharon knew the hours would be long when I hired her,' was the clipped reply.

Greg got to his feet, pulling Sharon up with him. 'All set, Keith? Anything else you need to know?'

They all went out of the front door where Greg's car was parked in the shade of one of the tall elms. He put his arms around Sharon and kissed her full on the mouth. 'See you tonight, Sharon.' Raising his head, he looked Ross straight in the eye. 'Don't work too hard, little brother—after all, there's not much point, is there? Ready, Keith?'

One last squeeze of her hips and he released Sharon, getting into his car and accelerating without a backward glance. Unconsciously Sharon let out her pent-up breath. Before she did anything she'd go and have a shower: scrub the feel of Greg's hands from her body.

Like a steel manacle, a hand encircled her arm and pulled her around so roughly that her braid flipped over her shoulder. Numbly she stared up at Ross, wishing the ground would open up and swallow her, or that by some miracle she could be transported a thousand miles away. His eyes were glittering with rage. He snarled, 'So what was that all about, Sharon?'

If only she could tell him ... She said weakly, 'Nothing. Greg and I are going out tonight, that's all.'

'Who the hell are you trying to kid?' He shook her as if she were a rag doll. 'What were you letting him paw you for? Don't tell me you were enjoying it!'

Greg's voice echoed in her ears: if you tell him, the deal's off. 'And why shouldn't I?' she lied boldly. 'Greg's a good-looking man. I'm looking forward to this evening.'

'I don't believe you,' he said coldly. 'Something's up, Sharon, isn't it? Tell me what it is.'

She looked him straight in the eye. 'Perhaps I've had enough of all this.' She gave the farmyard and the barns a disparaging glance. 'Don't forget I'm basically a city girl, Ross. Greg will show me a good time—that's all.'

For a moment she thought he was going to strike her and automatically she recoiled. 'I couldn't believe my eyes when I walked in and saw the two of you cuddled up so cosily on the chesterfield,' Ross grated. He stared into her eyes with all the force of his personality. 'Sharon, I still can't believe that the woman on the chesterfield is the real you.'

This was worse than she could possibly have anticipated. Somehow she had to end it ... 'You're the one who told me that in a matter of weeks you'd be turned off Marshwinds and left without a livelihood,' she said coolly. 'Maybe I've finally heard you. Greg's a wealthy man, Ross—I'm not immune to that.' She shrugged. 'Money's a very useful commodity, as I'm sure you'd agree, and I can use it as well as the next one.'

'So in return for a few more clothes and a diamond or two you'll get into Greg's bed,' he rasped. 'Because don't fool yourself, Sharon—a few kisses won't satisfy Greg.'

It was as if his words were actual physical blows, bruising her flesh. 'It won't be the first time a woman's done that, will it?'

'But I never thought you would.' He searched her

face with his eyes. 'This is all wrong—it's an act on your part, Sharon, I know it is. Has Greg got some sort of a hold over you? You can tell me what it is—I, of all people, should know what he's capable of. Just tell me the truth, that's all I ask.'

Quite literally she felt as though her heart was breaking. Ross was right: it was all an act. But she could not tell him the truth. Instead she had to convince him she was everything she was not. 'Maybe you don't really know me very well, Ross,' she said with just the right lack of emphasis. 'Greg and I will get along fine together. He's got money to spend and he likes a good time.'

'So you're just like the rest of them—a mercenary little bitch out for all you can get. How disappointed you must have been when you realised I didn't own Marshwinds! That I wasn't the rich man you'd thought I was.' His grin was savage. 'Didn't take you long to find an alternative, did it? You even kept it in the family—how nice.'

'Don't, Ross!' The words were jerked from her.

'So you have trouble accepting the truth, do you, Sharon? You should have thought of that sooner, shouldn't you?' He laughed mirthlessly. 'The ironic part of all this is that I was finally coming to trust in you. To believe I'd found a woman who was honest and loving and beautiful, a woman I could share my life with, with all the sorrows and the joys, the hard work and the fun. I looked at you and saw the mother of my children, the woman who would stand by my side no matter what happened.' He dropped her arm as if the contact was suddenly repugnant to him. 'I couldn't have been more wrong, could I? Although I suppose it's better to find out now than later.'

"Why did you never say any of this before?' she whispered. Her throat felt as raw as if she had shouted the words; her body ached all over.

'I'd have thought it was obvious. As you put it so succinctly a few minutes ago, I'm going to be turned off Marshwinds and left without a livelihood. Not much of a marital prospect, am I?'

'You mean you were thinking of marrying me?' Dimly she wondered if she was going to faint.

'Yes, exactly so ... well, you don't have to worry about it now. Because in the last couple of hours, I've changed my mind,' he replied cynically. 'You know, it really isn't fair, Sharon. You have the looks of an angel, and under all that beauty there's the soul of an avaricious little moneygrubber. You and Greg should do well together.'

'We should, shouldn't we?' she said tonelessly, smothering an urge to break into peals of hysterical laughter, so far from the truth was Ross. 'I'm going to get changed and mix up some feed.'

He looked her up and down, his eyes lingering on the slender length of her legs and the swell of her breasts. 'No point in wasting that outfit on me, is there?' he drawled.

Sharon dug her nails into her palms to force back the flood of angry words on the tip of her tongue. She had begun this charade; now she had to carry through with it. 'None whatsoever.'

She turned away, feeling his eyes sear into her back, praying he would not touch her. If he did, she knew she would begin to cry: no force in the world would be able to hold back the tears. But he did not. Going into the house through the front door, she went straight to her room, closing the door behind her, and as she did so feeling the first tear slide down her cheek. She flung herself on the bed, burying her head in the pillow to muffle the sound of her sobs, and cried her eyes out. For Ross, who had wanted to marry her and no longer did ... for herself who might well have lost her one chance of true happiness by trying to help the man she loved. ...

There were many times Sharon felt like crying as the July days passed by one by one, and Greg's presence became more and more of an intrusion in her life. She played her part valiantly. She endured kisses and embraces that left her inwardly shivering with revulsion; she laughed at his jokes and looked pleased to see him when he arrived to pick her up; she chatted artlessly to Ross about the fun she was having; and all the while her heart slowly died within her. No matter how strongly she tried to keep the goal of this exercise in mind, she began to feel more and more cheap, as though she was allowing herself to be used almost as a prostitute might. She was bitterly ashamed to be openly encouraging a man she despised to take physical liberties with her. With Ross she had gloried in physical contact, for it had opened up a whole new dimension for her; with Greg, however, she felt sullied and dirty. She began to lose weight. Her eyes grew permanently shadowed and bruised-looking, her voice brittle. She jumped at the slightest sound.

It was no consolation whatsoever to realise she was not alone in her misery. It had not taken Jock long to size up the situation; he had treated her at first with a kind of incredulous hostility which had gradually merged into an ignoring of her as if she no longer existed. At first she had tried to keep relations friendly between them, her eyes pleading with him for understanding; but all he saw was that Ross was being hurt, so that her tentative efforts at friendliness met with either an icy politeness or a frigid silence. Eventually she gave up trying.

Ross, too, had obviously decided to deal with the whole situation by ignoring it as much as was humanly possible. He exchanged no more words with Sharon than were absolutely necessary because of the demands of their work, and most of the time he managed to be elsewhere whenever Greg arrived. But this did not always happen, and when he was present to see Greg's proprietorial handling of Sharon and her own apparent pleasure, the girl would feel as though she was being flayed by the bitter contempt in his eyes.

She was desperately worried about him, for she knew he was driving himself mercilessly as his days at Marshwinds dwindled in number. Convinced, as he had to be, that Keith Hastings would be taking over the place in a matter of days, there was no sense to it, no logical reason why he should work from dawn until dusk. But with that sure intuitive knowledge she had of him, she could understand why he did: it made the hours pass, for one thing. But more than that, it was the only way he had of expressing his love for the place he was so soon to lose.

The weather was no help to anyone. Hot day followed glaringly hot day, the brassy sun high in a sky so bright that it hurt the eyes to look at it. There were no clouds nor the faintest stirrings of a breeze. The ground baked hard as clay. The grass beside the barns withered and dried. Tempers grew short and mistakes were made. And there were ten days left until Ross lost his option to buy Marshwinds. Nine days. Eight. . . .

For Sharon the passage of time brought at least one measure of relief. If the days were running out for Ross, so were they also for her and Greg. Greg would soon have to tell Keith Hastings the deal was off, and offer Ross Marshwinds at a price he could afford. She longed for the moment when this would take place. It was the only possible salve for the tension that had built within her to a screaming pitch. Every nerve in her body felt so tightly wound that even the slightest unexpected noise made her start as if someone had fired a gun behind her.

Everything had been leading up to the accident that finally happened on the evening of a particularly hot and sultry day. Ross had been overseeing some repairs in the chicken barn, which was temporarily empty; Sharon was outside waiting for Greg, who was to take her to a party at the summer home of one of his business associates in Chester. Part of Greg's ploy had been to buy her an entire wardrobe of new clothes; he had insisted on accompanying her to the shops and boutiques, an experience humiliating enough in itself. Worse than that, he had insisted that her purchases suit his own taste, so that everything she wore when she was with him was, to her eyes, slightly off key. A touch too tight, or too skimpy, or too harshly coloured. So now as she sat on the bench by the house in the shade of the elms she was wearing an electric blue dress of some kind of shiny fabric, with a deep décolletage and a skirt that was, to put it mildly, well fitting. In a gesture of rebellion, for Greg liked elaborate hairdos, she had left her hair loose and straight down her back, and her make-up was far more restrained than he would care for. She sat quietly, absently picking out the individual songs of the birds: the thin peep of the juncos, the belligerent churr of a red-winged blackbird, the melodic harmonies of the bobolinks that hovered over the meadows. But her fingers were restlessly smoothing the material of her dress, her air of repose a misnomer. When distantly from the hill there came the sound of a car engine she sat a little straighter, almost as if girding herself for battle. A few minutes later the car turned into the driveway and drew up in front of her with a flourish. Greg got out. 'Sorry I'm a bit late—got held up at the office.' He drew her to her feet and she stood unresistingly as he kissed her at some length; dimly she was grateful that Ross was nowhere in sight and did not have to see them. Greg drew back, a gleam of annoyance in his hazel eyes. 'Try a little harder, Sharon—you know what the conditions of our deal are.'

'I could hardly forget, the way you keep reminding me,' she retorted unwisely.

'Of course, if you don't want Ross to have Marshwinds——'

Cold fear clamped her heart in a vice-like grip. 'Don't talk that way! You know I've kept my side of the bargain.'

'Then you'll play it to the end, Sharon.'

It was an order, not a statement. She swallowed the hot torrent of words that welled up in her throat. 'I will,' she said evenly, her long-lashed eyes looking straight into his pale ones. 'After all, it's only for three or four more days.'

Something flickered in his eyes and was gone. 'Exactly. Ready to go?'

She bent to pick up her shawl, a gossamer-light affair of woven silk; as she did so, there came from the direction of the chicken barn, carried on the still evening air, a series of loud thuds and a bitten-off shout. Then silence, thick and absolute, almost as if she had dreamed the rest.

Frightened, she whispered, 'What was that?'

'Sounds as though something dropped—nothing to do with us,' Greg said impatiently. 'We'd better go, or we'll be late.'

The side door to the barn slid open and Doug came running across the grass towards them. Shaking off Greg's restraining hand, Sharon hurried to meet him, her high heels awkward on the rough ground. 'What is it, Doug?' she called.

'Bunch of lumber tipped over—landed on the boss,' Doug panted. He rarely walked anywhere, let alone ran: to him tractors and trucks, not legs, were the only sensible means of conveyance. 'Knocked him out. I'll get the truck and run him into the hospital.'

For the dour Doug this was a lot of words. Greg and the party and the deal they had made dropped out of Sharon's mind as if they had never existed. Ross was hurt ... she began to run, pulling up her skirt to give herself more freedom of movement, negotiating the uneven ground with instinctive skill, not even aware that Greg was following her. Bursting in the doorway to the barn, she stopped dead, momentarily unable to penetrate the gloomy interior after the sunlight outdoors. To her left she heard a muffled groan.

The floor was spread with clean shavings, the air not unpleasantly scented with disinfectant. Oblivious to all this, her eyes beginning to adjust to the dim light, Sharon saw a dark form lying on the floor amidst a clutter of fallen beams: Ross. She fell on her knees beside him, automatically feeling for his pulse. There was an ugly graze down one side of his face and already she could feel the swelling on his scalp under the thick hair, where the board must have struck him. She moved her fingers lightly over the rest of his head, then down his limbs, unconsciously letting out her breath in a sigh of relief as she discovered no evidence of broken bones or other damage.

He muttered something unintelligible under his breath, stirring restlessly. She put her palm flat on his chest, gently pushing back his hair with her other hand, her fingers cool on his forehead. 'Lie still,' she told him. 'Doug's gone to get the truck.'

Something must have penetrated the confusion in his brain. His eyes flickered open. 'Sharon?'

'Yes, it's me,' she answered ungrammatically, even in the stress of the moment noticing how the warmth of his skin spread into her palm; it had been such a long time since they had touched each other that even this tiny contact was like food after starvation, filling her with nameless longings. 'Doug's gone to get the truck,' she repeated clearly. 'You'll have to go into the hospital. Just for a check, to be on the safe side.'

'No need.'

'Yes, there is. It's all right, I'll go with you.'

He brought his hand up to lie clumsily across hers on his chest, wincing a little at the movement. His voice was so faint she could scarcely distinguish what he said, but she was sure she heard the words, thin and thread-like, '. . . missed you.' Oh God, she thought, her head bowed, I've missed you too, Ross, you'll never know how much. . . .'

Voices came from behind her, Doug saying gruffly, 'You'll have to give me a hand lifting him into the truck,' Greg's impatient reply, 'Well, hurry up, man—I haven't got all day.'

Sharon had to hide a smile, knowing Doug would be totally unimpressed by Greg's blustering, and indeed would probably move even more slowly than usual as a result of it. She said in a carefully neutral voice, oblivious of how her agonised pose of a moment ago had given her away, 'I think it's just a relatively minor concussion. No broken bones that I can see. But he should have an X-ray to be sure.'

'Don't know how he came to do it—boss isn't usually careless like that,' said Doug with gloomy relish.

Sharon knew all too well the pressures that had been on Ross lately, and felt such an upsurge of pure rage against Greg for his cold-blooded manipulation of Ross's life that for a moment she could not even speak, let alone look at him. She swallowed hard. 'If you bring that flat piece of board over, Doug, we can slide it under him and carry him out to the truck that way.'

The manoeuvre was accomplished with relative ease, for Ross seemed to have lapsed into unconsciousness again. Sharon took a malicious pleasure in seeing Greg get sawdust on the knees of his immaculate suit. It was hard to believe that in two or three days she would be free of him ... it couldn't be soon enough, for she did not think she had ever disliked anyone as much in her life as she disliked Greg. Dislike was too mild a word, she thought, as she helped guide the plank with Ross's recumbent form on it through the door. Despise. Loathe. Hate? She scarcely knew. She only knew that the release from this hateful artificial relationship with Greg would be every bit as powerful a relief as the lifting of the burden of suspicion at the hospital had been.

The back of Doug's truck was roofed in, doubling as a camper. The two men slid Ross's body in. Sharon said lightly, 'Give me a hand, Doug—I'll get in with him.'

Greg grabbed her arm. 'Oh, no, you won't!'

Her head swung round, her nostrils flaring. 'What do you mean—I won't?'

'I mean just what I say. You're going to the Creswells' party with me tonight, and we're already late.'

'Greg, I'm sorry about the party. But this is an emergency——'

He pulled her away from the truck, for Doug was listening to their exchange with undisguised interest. In a low voice that was rough with anger, he snarled, 'You've done your Florence Nightingale act, and very charming it was, too. But now you're coming with me.'

She tried to twist free, her breast heaving. 'Ross is hurt,' she choked. 'I have to go with him.'

'Your heroics are no doubt very touching, Sharon, but they're quite unnecessary. He's got a thick skull—he'll survive.'

She closed her eyes, fighting to clear her brain. 'You can follow us in the car. The hospital's not much out of our way, and once he's there, I'll come with you.'

'No.' His fingers dug into her arm. 'You'll come with me now or our deal's off. Is that clear?'

Appalled, she stared up at him. 'You wouldn't——'

'Try me.'

She dared not jeopardise their bargain now, not when it was so near completion and had cost her so dearly. Feeling physically sick, her knees trembling, she said tonelessly, 'Very well, I'll come with you now. But I'll never forgive you for this, Greg. Don't you realise that basically you're the one who's responsible for the accident in the first place? If you hadn't been causing Ross so much anxiety, he'd never have done anything so stupid as to let a bunch of boards fall on him.'

Greg laughed coarsely. 'If Ross can't handle a little pressure, that's his problem, not mine. Let's go.'

'Let go of my arm first.'

Under the cold-eyed directness of her stare, Greg's eyes fell. He dropped her arm, saying sullenly, 'Hurry up. There'll be some important people at that party, so I don't want to be late.'

Totally ignoring him, Sharon walked back over to the truck, where Doug was ostentatiously looking the other way. To his black-browed profile she said clearly, 'I have to go with Greg. You'll drive carefully, won't you, Doug?' In spite of herself, her voice quivered. 'I'll try and phone the hospital later this evening to see how he is.'

'I'll close the back of the truck, then,' Doug said impassively.

Together they walked round to the rear of the vehicle. Ross had not stirred, his eyes shut, his scraped, dirty face immobile. Very briefly Sharon rested her hand on his ankle, feeling her heart contract with love and pain. Her place was with him, not with Greg. She should be at his side now, when he needed her. And instead she was going to a party with a man she despised, to meet people she was not the slightest bit interested in meeting. It was all wrong. . . .

'Come on Sharon.'

Numbly she let go of Ross, giving Doug a wan smile to which he did not respond. Feeling tears crowd into her eyes, she turned away, stumbling across towards Greg's car, not even bothering to look and see if Greg was following her. She heard the metallic creak and slam of the truck doors, then the revving up of its engine, and still she walked steadily towards the car. By the time she was seated and Greg had joined her, the truck had driven away. It was too late now. The decision was made. . . .

As Greg inserted the key in the ignition, he said with lazy finality, 'You will not phone the hospital this evening, Sharon, nor will you phone Jock for news. You will act as if nothing has happened, and you will make an effort to at least look as though you're enjoying yourself.'

She lifted her chin haughtily, disdaining to reply, nor did she address a single word to him during the entire journey to Chester. It was a charming little town on the sea-coast, and at any other time she would have enjoyed exploring its winding streets and walking on its jetties. But her whole being was so focussed on getting through the evening and going home to Marshwinds that she could have been anywhere. Their host's house was a marvel of modernity and expense, the food and drink were copious and of the best quality, and a number of the guests were potentially very interesting people; but like a robot Sharon moved through the hours, responding politely to the conversations with no idea afterwards of what she had said, meeting people whose faces and names then dropped completely out of her mind, drinking rather more vodka than was good for her. Twice she had tried to get to the telephone, even getting as far as looking up the number of the hospital in the phone book, but each time Greg had followed her, putting his arm around her with false geniality and drawing her back into the party. A small band arrived. There was dancing and more food, delicious lobster patties served with salad and crisp, hot rolls, followed by strawberry shortcake laden with whipped cream and fresh berries. Coffee and cognac. More dancing. Then finally, blessedly, people started to leave. It was two in the morning.

Once back in the car, Sharon closed her eyes. Thank goodness that was over, she thought in mute gratitude. Now she could go home. She had a dull, throbbing headache, aftermath of tension and too much to drink; the car's smooth rhythm was soothing, and imperceptibly she drifted off to sleep.

She did not waken until the car braked and made a sharp turn, the signal light clicking. A turn to the right? It should have been to the left, she thought confusedly, opening her eyes and blinking in the glare of lights. They were parked, not in front of the farmhouse, but in front of a garishly lit motel, its red sign flashing the message that there were vacancies still available. Her throat closed in panic. 'Where are we?' she stammered, her voice still blurred with sleep.

'We're going to book a room here.'

'No!' She fumbled with the door latch.

'Stop that, Sharon, and listen to me.' Unwillingly her head swung round at the note of command in Greg's voice; momentarily he had sounded like Ross. 'Nothing's going to happen.' His eyes slid over her derisively. 'I did telephone Marshwinds this evening. Ross is back home, they didn't keep him at the hospital. I want this to be the finishing touch—that you and I stayed out all night. He'll draw all the obvious conclusions, of course.'

'I'll deny it.'

'Go ahead—and good luck to you.'

She bit her lip, knowing what she would believe were she in Ross's shoes. 'I have to get back for the milking,' she said stubbornly.

'So you will—three hours from now.' He paused. 'I'm going to register. Don't try anything silly, will you, Sharon? We both know I hold all the cards.'

The three hours they spent in the motel room were to seem like the longest in Sharon's life. She was too strung up to sleep again, so she sat tensely in the chair by the mirrored dresser, memorising the undistinguished contents of the room for want of anything better to do. Months later the mere sight of a carpet in that particular bilious shade of green would have the power to induce in her a wave of frustration and helplessness so strong that she could have been back in the room. Greg stretched out on the bed, arms linked behind his head, smoking cigarette after cigarette. She should be grateful, she supposed, that he made no advances on her; she had some time ago concluded that she was safe from him in that sense, for her initial refusal of him had damaged his male ego sufficiently that he would not risk rejection again; instead he chose to regard her with a contempt that was laced with dislike.

Everything, no matter how disagreeable, has to come to an end sooner or later. Greg got up from the bed, stubbed out his cigarette in the ashtray, and then crumpled the bedclothes realistically. 'That should do, don't you think, Sharon? Ready to go?' He picked up his jacket, slinging it across his shoulder, not bothering to do up his collar or straighten his tie. All part of the act, the girl thought wearily. That it would be convincing she did not for a moment doubt.

The sun was up over the horizon by the time they reached Marshwinds, the sky flushed with pink. Dew sparkled on the grass while the birds carolled with insensate joy. A beautiful day, Sharon thought numbly as Greg parked the car, not at all surprised to see Ross come out of the house and walk towards them. There was a patch of plaster on his cheekbone; as he came closer she could see the other abrasions and bruises on his face. He held himself rigidly upright. His eyes were a brilliant blue, hard as glass, and she knew they were missing not one detail of the couple in the car: Greg's unusual dishabille, her own obvious weariness. 'So,' he drawled, 'you're back. Nice of you to return her in time for work, Greg—or were you already tired of her?'

'Far from it, little brother. But I'll be seeing her again tonight, and tomorrow night. . . .' Greg let his voice trail of suggestively.

Sharon saw the muscles twitch in Ross's jaw. She got out of the car, saying evenly, 'I'm going to get changed. Goodbye, Greg.'

'See you tonight, honey. Usual time.'

Sharon walked towards the house, letting herself in

the back door. The kitchen, thank heavens, was empty, although the odour of bacon and coffee lingered, filling her throat with the bitter taste of nausea. She fought it down and went to her room.

It was all so familiar, and yet she felt a million miles away from the comfort and security it had once represented. She unstrapped her shoes and unzipped her dress, letting it fall on the floor. She would never wear it again, she knew that. On impulse she went into the bathroom, bundling her hair under a shower cap, and stepping under the stinging spray of hot water, as if by physical means she could wash off the sordid misery of the long night. Turning off the taps, she pulled off the cap, shaking her hair free, and wrapped a towel around her. Still moving as if in a dream, she went back into the bedroom.

And there the dream ended, for Ross was standing by the bed waiting for her. Now that she saw him she knew she had subconsciously been expecting him to be there. She said steadily, her fingers clasped at her breast to hold the towel in place, 'I don't expect you to believe this, but I have not made love with Greg, nor will I ever make love with him.'

His smile was so ugly that she winced. 'What a splendid actress you are, Sharon! The wronged female, done to perfection. Your talents have been wasted as a nurse and a farm worker—you really should be on the stage.'

There seemed to be nothing she could say to this. He took two steps closer, so there could be no mistaking the contemptuous fury in his eyes. In an almost conversational tone of voice, he went on, 'You're just a promiscuous little bitch, aren't you? Selling yourself to the highest bidder.' Her white-faced silence only infuriated him further. He took her by the shoulders, noticing with savage pleasure how her hand tightened on the towel and how fear flickered across her taut features. 'What are you frightened of?' he taunted. 'I can't imagine I could be a less sensitive lover than Greg.'

She said rudely, 'You're not going to have the chance to find out.'

'No?' he answered silkily. He lowered his head with a deliberate slowness and brushed her lips with his own, then slid his mouth down her neck to the bottom of her throat. Her skin was warm and sweetly scented from the shower, and it took only her tiny movement backwards from him to make him lose control. As if it was happening to another woman, Sharon felt herself being lifted and flung on the bed, the towel falling open. Frantically she tried to cover herself. Then he was on top of her, hard bone and muscle forcing her back, mouth a brutal demand. With all her strength she wrenched her head free. 'No, Ross!' she gasped. 'No! It's wrong this way——'

Her protest undammed his anger. 'You couldn't even come to the hospital with me, could you? I mean that little to you!'

'Greg wouldn't let me. Oh, Ross, you don't understand——' Her broken voice was a plea in itself. 'I wanted to—you must believe me!' Suddenly, perhaps taking both of them by surprise, all the tensions Sharon had endured over the past few hours erupted in a storm of weeping. She twisted sideways, smothering her face in the mattress, her shoulders shaking as her throat was convulsed by sobs that seemed to tear her apart.

Dimly she heard Ross mutter, 'Oh, for Pete's sake!'

His weight was lifted from her, and she shoved a fist into her mouth in an effort to quell her frantic crying. 'I—I'm sorry,' she quavered.

'I've had enough of this.' His words fell like drops of ice-water on her over-heated skin, so cold and unfeeling were they. 'Get dressed and go down to the barn, Sharon. In a week's time this place won't be mine any more, so as of now I'm giving you a week's notice. What you do then is up to you. You can move in with Greg. You can go back to Montreal. I don't give a damn. Just as long as you're not around me!'

Her breath caught in her throat in a new wave of pain. When the door clicked shut, she raised a tear-streaked face. She was alone in the room. The room that, according to Ross, would be hers for only a few more nights. She sat up, scrubbing at her eyes. Only a

few short weeks ago this place had beckoned to her like
a home, promising her a welcome and a warmth she
had been lacking all her life . . . but it had been a false
promise, she knew that now. The tide had gone out,
leaving her stranded on the beach amongst her
shattered hopes and dreams.

CHAPTER NINE

Two days passed. Ross ignored Sharon with a
thoroughness that at any other time she might have
found faintly amusing; she felt instead as though a part
of her had been amputated, and that she would never
be whole again. Jock maintained his pose of frosty
politeness; Doug, of course, kept up his usual dour
silences: that at least had not changed. Between one day
and the next the sunshine vanished, the steady,
drenching rains alleviating at least one source of tension
at Marshwinds. But for the rest Sharon felt as though
she was living on a minefield, where at any time a
violent explosion could erupt, shattering the quiet for
her, it was nothing but an illusion to start with.

The explosion, when it did come, was from a totally
unexpected quarter. Greg had taken her to his club for
dinner. It was ladies' night; the high-ceiling rooms were
filled with the murmur of well-bred conversation, the
clink of glasses, the glitter of diamonds. Automatically
Sharon went through her routine, scarcely even noticing
any more when Greg's heavy hand would fall on her
shoulder or his arm would encircle her waist. She made
all the appropriate responses to the people she met,
produced some reasonably intelligent conversation
herself, sipped her admittedly excellent sherry, and
longed for it all to be over. It was not until after dinner,
when Greg had disappeared somewhere, that she came
face to face with Keith Hastings. He stared at her,
plainly trying to place her. 'Sharon Reid,' she said
obligingly. 'I met you at Marshwinds Farm—I work for

Ross Bowen.' In these distinguished surroundings it gave her an obscure pleasure to be so blunt, because she was quite sure no one else in the room was working for the minimum wage.

'Ah, yes, I remember.' He raised his glass, which, judging by the unfocussed look in his eyes, was far from his first. 'You must congratulate me, Miss Reid. In exactly four days, Marshwinds will be mine.'

She stared at him blankly. 'I beg your pardon?'

'The papers are all drawn up—in fact, Greg and I had a get-together about it today. Of course, nothing can be formalised until the last of the month, because of the terms of the will. But all it will take is a couple of signatures—and a cheque, naturally!' He laughed heartily at his own wit.

'I think you must be making a mistake, Mr Hastings,' she said with careful precision, putting her glass down on a nearby table. 'You see, I happen to know for a fact that Greg is planning to sell the farm to Ross, after all. He's going to withdraw the offer to you.'

Keith Hastings patted her shoulder patronisingly. 'No, no, my dear—it's all settled, you're quite mistaken. Anyway, you shouldn't be bothering your pretty little head over these matters. Leave them to me and Greg.'

Coldly furious, she reiterated obstinately, 'Greg's going to sell Marshwinds to Ross, for a quarter of a million dollars.'

'And miss out on half a million?' Keith laughed again, taking a long drink. 'Don't you kid yourself, Sharon. Greg wouldn't pass up that amount of money, not for any family sentiments. Not that he has many as far as his half-brother's concerned.'

Sharon tried to fight down the paralysing conviction that Keith Hastings was telling the truth, saying as calmly as she could, 'But nothing's really settled yet, is it? Greg can't sell you Marshwinds until the first day of August.'

'True enough. But everything else has been done. Legal work, deed searches, documents all drawn up and ready to sign. And I've made all the financial arrangements—the money's as good as Greg's, and he knows it.'

It *was* the truth. It had to be. Greg had gone ahead with all the plans to sell Marshwinds to Keith Hastings. The inevitable corollary of this was, of course, that he had had no intentions whatsoever of selling to Ross at the reduced price; that, just as he had been playing games with Ross all this time, so he had also been playing games with her. Stringing her along. Knowing all the time that at the last minute he was going to back out of their bargain. And what protection did she have? None whatsoever. Nothing in writing, Greg had said. Now that it was too late she knew she should have insisted on some actual record of their deal, because without it, she was powerless. A credulous victim of a man without scruples or ethics: from his treatment of Ross she should have known that.

All these thoughts flashed rapidly through her mind. She said bitterly, 'I'll certainly not drink to your acquisition of Marshwinds, Mr Hastings. Because you know as well as I do that when you buy Marshwinds, you're dispossessing a man from a place he loves. A place he's worked for, body and soul. A finer man than you, or Greg, could ever hope to be.' She nodded at him coolly. 'Good evening.'

She turned and in a leisurely fashion surveyed the room, searching among the well-dressed crowd and the uniformed waiters for Greg. It did not take long to locate him. He was standing by the door with a group of men, expansively waving a cigar in the air, his fleshy face flushed as he recounted what she was willing to bet was an off-colour story. Her jaw set grimly, she began threading her way purposely through the crowd. Touching him on the sleeve to get his attention, she said without finesse, 'I have to talk to you.' She smiled with artificial sweetness at his companions. 'Something urgent—a matter of business. I'm sure you'll excuse us.'

Greg glanced quickly at her set profile. 'Honey, can't it——'

'No.'

He shrugged with attempted good humour. 'I'll be

back in a minute,' he said, allowing himself to be steered into the lofty foyer where an immense gilt chandelier did little to alleviate the gloom of the dark mahogany panelling. With exaggerated patience he said, 'What is it, Sharon?'

'We're leaving. Right now.'

'Don't be silly——'

'Because if we don't, I shall make a scene such as this place has never witnessed before.' There were bright patches of colour high in her cheeks. 'In front of all your friends. You wouldn't want me to do that, would you, Greg?'

Whatever his faults, Greg was not a stupid man: one look at her face was enough to convince him she meant every word she said. Sullenly he capitulated, 'Come on, then.'

Once in the car she said with crystal clarity, 'We'll drive back to Marshwinds now, Greg, and you'll tell Ross about the deal you and I made, and you'll give him a formal, written statement to the effect that he can buy the place for a quarter of a million.'

As Greg thoughtfully turned the key in the ignition, her heart began to race in her breast at the expression on his face. 'Just like that, eh?'

'Yes.'

He laughed, pulling out of the parking lot and into the street. 'I'll take you back to the farm, if that's where you want to go.'

The silence stretched out between them. Sharon said tightly, 'And what about the rest?'

'No dice, honey.' With patent insincerity, he added as an afterthought, 'Sorry.'

'Are you telling me the deal's off?'

'Yeah ... it never really was on, Sharon. I just thought it would be fun to string you and Ross along.'

Angrier than she had ever been in her life before, she seethed, 'I was talking to Keith Hastings and he told me everything was in order for him to buy the place. In my naïveté I thought he was making a mistake.'

'Too bad, honey. In four days Marshwinds will belong to Keith. I don't know why you're making such a fuss—Keith's willing to keep Ross on as a foreman for at least a month. He'll have to move out of the house, but that shouldn't be any problem.'

'You know Ross will never stay on like that!' she retorted passionately. 'So all along you never meant a word of what you said to me. You had no intention of selling Marshwinds to Ross.'

They were driving over the newer of the two bridges that spanned the harbour, the curving indentation of Bedford Basin to their left, its shores spangled with lights. 'Of course not—what kind of a fool do you think I am?' The suave and goodhumoured mask had vanished; there was naked brutality in his voice. 'You were the fool, to believe me. I didn't think you'd fall for it, but I figured it was worth a try. And then you did . . . but of course you're so head over heels in love with Ross, you'd do anything for him, wouldn't you?'

'My feelings for Ross are my own business,' she returned coldly. She closed her eyes, trying to think, as Greg whipped in and out of the two lanes of traffic. Her whole soul rose up in revolt at the thought of asking Greg for anything, particularly when she was ninety-nine per cent sure he wouldn't do it, but she had to try. Forcing herself to sound passably humble, she said, 'Will you at least tell Ross what was going on? So he'll know why you and I were going out together?'

He laughed outright. 'No.'

'Please. . . .'

'What's in it for me, Sharon?'

'Nothing, I suppose.' She added nastily, 'Unless it would be the knowledge that belatedly you'd done one small thing that was honest and decent.'

'You should know me better than that.'

He was so thoroughly smug, so intolerably self-satisfied. Unable to bear looking at him, Sharon stared out of the window as the miles whipped by, her feelings in a turmoil. At first her predominant emotion was one of mere relief: no longer would she have to maintain the façade of going out with Greg and supposedly enjoying his company. She'd give away every single article of clothing he'd ever bought for her, she decided viciously.

But as they left the rocky environs of the city and the land grew more and more pastoral, gently sloping fields gradually replacing lakes and spruce bogs, her relief was increasingly diluted by anxiety. Sure, she could tell Ross of her abortive attempt to save the farm—but would he believe her? Would she, in his shoes? If he didn't, then it meant that not only was Marshwinds lost, but his good opinion of her was gone for ever, and with it any hope that he might marry her. . . .

They had reached the outskirts of the little town where she had asked Steve to let her off so many weeks ago. With a peculiar poignancy she found herself wondering if she wouldn't have been better off if he had done so. Then she would never have arrived at Marshwinds and never met Ross . . . as if her thoughts had conjured him up, she saw a white Mercedes parked on the side of the street. 'Stop, Greg,' she demanded breathlessly. 'Isn't that Ross's car?'

He pulled over, saying in a peculiar voice, 'I do believe you're right. Yes, it's his licence number.' He gave a snort of laughter. 'Looks to me as though brother Ross is drowning his sorrows in drink.'

'What do you mean?' Her voice was sharp.

'He's parked outside the tavern.'

He was right. The bright neon sign flashed on and off monotonously. The windows were shuttered so none of the passers-by could see in, giving the place a secretive, somehow sinister, air. 'Ross wouldn't be in there,' she said uncertainly.

'He rarely drinks at home, because of Jock,' Greg replied impatiently. 'And there's one way for us to find out if he's in there, and that's to go in.'

To be seen once more by Ross in Greg's company? 'You don't have to come. I'll go in alone.'

'I wouldn't miss this for the world,' he said smoothly.

'If Ross was indeed inside trying to find a kind of temporary oblivion, the last thing he needed was Greg gloating over him. 'You're not going in there, Greg.'

He chucked her indulgently under the chin, ignoring the force behind her proscription. 'You can't stop me, honey.'

'If you go in there with me, tomorrow I'll write a letter to the president of your club describing our little bargain and your last-minute retraction.'

'You can't do that—you've got no proof.'

'No, I haven't, and I'll make that clear in the letter. But it should cause some rather interesting gossip, shouldn't it?'

'You little bitch!'

She threw back her head and laughed. 'What a marvellous double standard you have, Greg! The trouble is, I've been spending too much time with you lately, I'm starting to pick up your methods.' Abruptly she sobered. 'I hope I never have to see you again, Greg Bowen. I find it very difficult to forgive you for what you've done to Ross and to me.' There was nothing else to say. 'Goodbye,' she added, with absolute finality.

She got out of the car, slamming the door shut behind her with a sense of freedom regained; whatever else happened, she was through with all the horrible falsities of the liaison with Greg. Drawing her shawl around her shoulders, she walked across the sidewalk and pushed open the heavy swing door.

The fetid air hit her like a blast—warm, stale, smelling of beer and cigarette smoke and sweat. She blinked, trying to adjust her eyes to the dim light, holding tightly to the edges of her shawl. The dress she was wearing was full-skirted with cap sleeves and a rather charmingly cut bodice; as a battery of male eyes swivelled around to look at her, she was suddenly glad she was not wearing the tight blue dress that had been another of Greg's purchases. There were some women in the tavern, she saw gratefully, but they were few and far between, and they were not alone. A waiter brushed past her carrying a tray loaded with draught beer; Sharon stepped inside, her eyes running over the tables in a vain search for Ross.

From the nearest table a man called thickly, 'Looking for someone, baby? You can join us.'

He was thickset, the belly straining at his singlet mute evidence of too many evenings spent in the tavern. But his eyes were not unkind. She said clearly, 'I'm looking for Ross Bowen. Do you know if he's here?'

One of the other men spoke up. 'He's in the other room, miss.' He cleared his throat awkwardly. 'He's been there a while. Are you sure——'

She favoured him with a generous smile that made him redden appreciatively. 'Thanks.' Threading her way through the crowded, noisy room with more assurance now that she knew where she was going, she reached the far room and stood in the doorway.

She saw Ross immediately. He was sitting alone at a small table pushed against the wall. There was a half-empty glass as well as a full one in front of him; he was staring down at the table top. Despite the convivial atmosphere of the tavern, she could understand why he sat alone: there was something forbidding in that still figure, an unspoken message of self-imposed isolation that would have discouraged any but the most thick-skinned from joining him. She took a deep breath, and with no idea what she was going to say, walked across the room, pulled out the second chair at his table, and sat down.

His features were blurred, the blue eyes out of focus. He said nastily, his words slurred, 'Well, look who's here—Florence Nightingale!'

She could not afford to let the hurt show. She said evenly, 'Ross, let's go home.'

Her choice of words was unfortunate. 'But it's not home, is it, Sharon? Not for me, any more. And it never was for you.'

'Jock will be worried about you.'

'Jock's gone to visit an old Navy buddy who lives in Annapolis. Otherwise do you think I'd be doing this?'

Her heart ached for him. Proud, self-sufficient Ross, driven to seek forgetfulness in a noisy, crowded beer parlour. 'Let me at least drive you back to Marshwinds. You shouldn't drive as you are.'

Greg would have blustered and argued with her; Ross merely said, 'I was planning to take a taxi.' Without any visible change of expression, he added, 'Where's Greg?'

'He's gone back to Halifax. I won't be seeing him any more.'

'Oh? Tired of you, is he?'

Her lashes flickered. She knew it was beyond her to try and explain the whole sorry mess to Ross now, in this place—not that she had any guarantee that he would even listen. 'Let's go,' she repeated patiently.

Very slowly he levered himself upright, leaning on the table, his knuckles taught with strain. She too stood, fighting back a wave of compassion as she saw beads of sweat form on his forehead. With an intense effort of will he straightened to his full height, swaying slightly. Sharon knew better than to offer help. Without looking back to see if he was behind her, she began to walk back the way she had come, on her way to the door passing the table where she had asked for Ross; the thickset man raised his glass to her in a salute. 'Found him, eh? Lucky guy—I'd go home with you any day.'

She flushed, hearing Ross's sharply indrawn breath. To distract him, she said quickly, holding the door open for him, 'May I have the car keys?'

He fumbled in his pocket, holding them out for her. 'Who was that guy?'

'When I first went in, I asked him if you were there— I couldn't see you.'

'What the hell was Greg thinking of, letting you go in that place by yourself?' His voice was thick with anger.

She unlocked the passenger's door on the Mercedes. 'I wouldn't let him go in with me,' she replied shortly. Had she been looking at Ross, she would have seen puzzlement cloud his eyes, as if he was struggling with an idea beyond his ken. But she was walking around the car to get in the driver's seat. She eased the Mercedes out on to the street, her attention concentrated on remembering the controls, and when she did eventually steal a sideways glance at her companion, he was leaning back in his seat, his eyes closed, the breeze through the open window ruffling his hair. Unawares, she was struck by a pang of love for him so strong that the car swerved momentarily. Fiercely she forced her mind back to her driving.

He had presumably noticed nothing amiss, and the rest of the drive was accomplished without mishap, although as Sharon pulled up in front of the house and turned off the engine, she found her wrists were weak with strain and knew it was not from the driving. It was both heaven and hell to have Ross in the car with her, she thought miserably: so near, yet so impossibly far away. She said in a voice that sounded almost normal, 'We're here, Ross.'

He said nothing. He got out of the car, preceding her across the grass towards the house; she had the impression he was putting his feet very carefully one in front of the other, for the usual economical grace with which he moved was totally lacking. Once in the kitchen, he stripped off his shirt, flinging it across the back of one of the chairs, and went over to the sink. Turning on the cold tap full blast, he ducked his head under it and held it there, dousing his arms and shoulders with the ice-cold water. Finally he turned the tap off, groping for the towel and roughly drying his face and hair. When he looked across at Sharon the clarity of full intelligence was back in the blue eyes. He looked her up and down. 'So . . .' he said slowly, 'here we are. Alone in the house.'

Her eyes widened fractionally. 'Jock?'

'Won't be back until tomorrow. It was high time he had a day away from here—I haven't been the easiest person in the world to live with lately. So we're quite alone, Sharon.'

Had there been the slightest warmth in his voice or in his expression, she would have welcomed such solitude, for there was no one else in the world she would rather be with. But he had spoken quite dispassionately, and there was a dangerous calm in the way he waited for her response. With an attempted lightness, not meeting his eyes, she said, 'You'd better get to bed or you won't be in any state for the milking tomorrow. I'm tired, too.'

'I am not at all tired, Sharon.' He walked around the table to stand in front of her; frozen to the spot, she stood her ground. 'It seems a shame to waste such an opportunity, don't you think?'

'Ross, I've had about all I can take for one evening,' she said jerkily. 'Please don't——'

'So you and Greg have really come to a parting of the ways?'

She nodded wordlessly.

'I fail to understand you, Sharon—you're turning your back on a lot of money. More than I'll ever have.'

'It wasn't the money!' she burst out. 'It never was.'

'Then what was it for—this?' His mouth stilled her words, his hands on her back drawing her close to the hard length of his body. There was no tenderness in the kiss, no concern for her needs. She fought against his demands, holding herself rigidly, her palms against his chest. But it had been too long since Ross had touched her and held her; even as she struggled against it, she felt warmth and the sweet, imperious ache of desire spread through her body, and she knew in some deep level of her being that she needed to erase all the ugly memories of Greg, to superimpose over them the wild beauty, the absolute rightness, of Ross's lovemaking. Her lips parted. As she felt the first touch of his mouth, she ran her hands up his chest to caress the thick, damp hair that curled at his nape. It was a kiss that seemed to go on for ever, and for Sharon it was peace and fulfilment after a long separation. When she felt herself being lifted, she offered no resistance, burying her face in his neck, feeling the hard curve of his collarbone against her cheek, the roughness of hair on her breast.

Ross put her down on the bed in a room she knew must be his; she gained a confused impression of whites and muted greens, of stark simplicity, an almost monastic bareness. Then within seconds he was on the bed beside her, stripped to a pair of brief shorts, the cleanly sculpted lines of his body taut and beautiful. Without haste he undid the thin straps on her high-heeled sandals, removing them from her feet, his fingers fondling her slimly boned feet and ankles. Every nerve she possessed came to life at his touch. Then his hands slid up her body, and again, with that absence of haste that was in itself a source of sensuality, he undid the fastenings on her dress, drawing it down over her hips and legs and dropping it to the floor. The two wisps of nylon and lace that were all that was left of her clothing revealed more than they concealed: they were a provocation in themselves. Still in utter silence, Ross began to stroke her breast, his face intent on what he was doing; Sharon did not think she had ever seen anything more lovely than the sight of his lean tanned fingers lying against the whiteness of her skin. She had forgotten everything but Ross and his need of her; Greg might never have existed. Without even having to think about it, she knew that with her body she could give Ross the gift of oblivion ... perhaps, if they were to make love, he would divine her unspoken comfort and love. It was all she could give him, she thought with a painful catch in her throat.

So when he began to kiss her again, his teeth nibbling at her lips, she responded with all the generosity of her nature, pressing herself close to him, her nails probing the hard muscles of his back. His hands were everywhere, caressing, stroking, seeking, demanding, awakening her to a fever pitch of excitement beyond anything she had ever experienced. That he was equally aroused, she could not help but know. Her heart beating with thick, heavy strokes, she felt her hips move under him in a rhythm that was instinctive, as old as time, wanting to gather him in and make him hers in the most primitive and real way there was. Forgetting that he still had not spoken a word, heedless that this could represent any kind of a threat to her, she murmured into his ear, pressing his face to her breast, 'Ross, I want you so much—I've never felt like this before.'

His hands grew still. She was suddenly aware of his weight, crushing her into the mattress. He raised his head and with a pang of pure terror she saw that he was angry, desire banished by a fury so intense that it burned like twin pinpoints in his eyes. '*What* did you say?' he demanded.

'I said I wanted you,' she faltered. 'What's wrong with that?'

'What else did you say?'

'That I'd never felt this way before.'

'So you never felt this way with Greg.' His teeth

white against his tanned face, he snarled, 'Is that why you're here now? He wasn't enough for you. He couldn't satisfy you, was that the trouble?'

For a moment she was too stunned to do anything but stare up at him, aghast. Then the meaning of his words, crude and inescapably ugly, penetrated her brain. Her eyes, that only moments before had been slumbrous with pleasure, darkened to purple with uncontrollable fury. Her hand reached out and caught him across the face, the sound of flesh on flesh shockingly loud.

She subsided on the bed, appalled by her own action, feeling pain shoot up her wrist, even as a red stain spread on his cheek. Yet how else could she have responded? 'That was a foul thing to say,' she choked.

'The truth hurts, doesn't it?' he taunted.

'Ross, I never slept with Greg——'

'Don't make me laugh! I saw the two of you together. I know you stayed at that motel. And then you have the nerve to tell me you didn't sleep with him!' He was looking at her as though he despised her; worse, as though he despised himself for being with her. 'I don't know what I'm doing here with you now,' he muttered. 'Heaven help me, part of me was pleased to see you walk into that tavern to find me.' He swung his legs round, sitting on the edge of the bed, his head buried in his hands.

Feeling as though she would shatter into pieces if she moved too quickly, Sharon fumbled with the closure on her bra. There was the sour taste of defeat in her mouth: Greg had won, and she had lost. All that was left was to retreat with as much dignity as she could. She reached for her dress, pulling it over her head and doing it up, her fingers stiff and awkward. Picking up her shoes, she padded on bare feet over to the door and let herself out. Risking one quick backwards glance, she saw that Ross was sitting in exactly the same place. He too was defeated, she thought with painful clarity; it was all there to be read in the downbent curve of his spine and the rounded shoulders. And there was nothing she could do to help. He was as far away from her as if there were a thousand miles between them.

CHAPTER TEN

SHARON went to her room and sat on the bed, her legs curled up underneath her in an effort to warm her cold feet. Not bothering to put on the light, she stared unseeingly into the darkness as the full extent of her loss began to dawn on her. She had lost Ross, that much was certain. She and Greg between them had done their work all too well; nothing would convince Ross now that she was innocent of any involvement with Greg. But more than that, she had lost any chance of saving Marshwinds for Ross. And without Marshwinds, even if by some miracle he did come to believe in her innocence, he would never ask her to marry him . . . he was too proud for that. So he was doubly lost to her.

Not even in the worst days at the hospital had Sharon ever been attacked so bitterly by the twin forces of loneliness and despair. She had received a blow too mortal for tears, a wound too deep to be healed by rationalisation or hope. In a very few days, indeed a matter of hours, she would be turned away from Marshwinds and from Ross; she would, she supposed, return to Montreal and there endeavour to forget him, to put behind her these enchanted weeks among the fields and orchards and barns. How she would do it, she had no idea, for in the wasteland that lay about her there was no hiding the unpalatable truth that the love she bore for Ross was deeply rooted in the very grounds of her being. To tear it up might well destroy her.

It was a long time before the girl moved, and then it was only to lie down under the covers, huddling under them for comfort. She might have slept fitfully; certainly she heard instantly the sounds of Ross getting up for the milking. She dressed quickly, almost glad to have something concrete to do, and hurried down to the meadow in the dawn light to bring in the cows. But it was not until she was guiding them into their stalls, Myrtle as usual insisting on going anywhere but in her own stanchion, that the idea hit Sharon. Perhaps—and this thought brought the first smile of the day to her lips—it was Myrtle's sheer perversity that reminded her of her mother and her grandmother; at any rate, she stood transfixed as Myrtle ambled unimpeded up the aisle and nonchalantly selected Sally's stall despite the fact that Sally was already in it.

'For heaven's sake, Sharon! Get that darned cow out of there!'

'Oh . . . oh, sorry,' she mumbled, grabbing a stick and belatedly guiding Myrtle in the right direction. But as she snapped Myrtle's collar into the chain on the stanchion, she was not thinking about the cow at all. She was thinking about Rowena. Rowena had money, and Ross needed money. But Rowena, she remembered only too well, had made it very clear the day of their first meeting that as a wealthy woman she was frequently importuned and disliked it very much. If she, Sharon, went asking for help for Ross, would that ruin the delicate balance of the new relationship between her and Rowena? For all its newness, it was a relationship she valued and did not want to damage. Yet Rowena was the only ray of hope in a situation that had seemed completely hopeless; for Ross's sake, she did not think she could leave any stone unturned.

She was in the utility room washing out the milk cans when Ross joined her there. 'I'm going down to the lower pasture,' he yelled above the roar of the vacuum pump. 'Fences need mending!'

Sharon nodded, glad for once to see him go. She raced through the rest of the chores, ran up to the house, showered, and put on her mauve dress. Then she went back to the kitchen. The car keys were on the shelf over the sink, where she had left them last night. She pocketed them and wrote Ross a note, saying simply that she had borrowed the car to visit her grandmother, she would be home after lunch. He would be furious, she knew, but at this stage in the game it did not seem to matter much. Hurrying outside, she glanced around quickly to see if Ross was in sight before sliding behind the wheel of the Mercedes.

She took the most direct route she knew to her grandmother's and drove as fast as the speed limit would allow, so that it was still relatively early in the morning when she drew up outside the vast Victorian edifice that Rowena called home. She got out of the car, walked up the steps and rang the bell. The same maid opened the door, although it did seem to Sharon that the girl had a shade more assurance this time. Once again there was the wait in the cool, panelled hall before Sharon was ushered into the sitting room at the back of the house. However, this time there was a warmly welcoming smile on the face of the white-haired figure sitting so uprightly in the wing-backed chair. 'Sharon! What a lovely surprise, dear. How are you?'

Sharon bent and kissed the faded cheek; this morning Rowena smelled rather wickedly of Yves St Laurent's most expensive perfume. Then she sat down rather abruptly in the same highly uncomfortable chair she remembered from her first visit. Now that she was here, she had no idea what she was going to say. Her grandmother was genuinely delighted to see her: no question of that. Would she be as delightful when she knew why Sharon had come? Importuned . . . the word seemed to reverberate in Sharon's brain. In an agony of indecision, she chewed her lip.

'Have you had breakfast?'

'Oh . . . er—no. But that's all right, I'm not hungry.'

But Rowena had picked up the silver bell on the Chinese console table beside her, and was ringing it. The maid appeared and breakfast was ordered. 'Now,' Rowena said placidly, folding her beringed hands in her lap, 'why don't you tell me what's wrong?'

'It's that obvious, is it?' the girl rejoined ruefully.

'Oh, yes. Is it to do with that very handsome but no doubt very difficult young man of yours?'

As a description of Ross, it could hardly help but amuse Sharon. She nodded, her fingers twisting the belt of her dress. 'Everything's such a mess, Rowena!' she burst out. 'I don't know what to do!'

'Begin by telling me about it.'

The girl blinked furiously, determined not to cry: dry and practical as her grandmother's voice might sound, Sharon was sensitive enough to discern the concern behind it. She said rapidly, before her courage could fail her, 'In three days' time Ross is going to lose Marshwinds,' she gulped. 'And he hates me—although maybe despises is a better word. He thinks I'm his half-brother's mistress, you see.'

Rowena leaned forward, obviously intrigued. 'No, I don't see at all. I had no idea life could be so interesting on a farm. Now, begin at the beginning, Sharon. Why is Ross going to lose Marshwinds? Is he selling it?'

Trying to marshal her thoughts into some kind of coherent order, Sharon plunged into the story of Ross's parenthood, Gerald's will, Greg's machinations. She was interrupted in the middle by the arrival of an exquisitely arranged tray of melon and scrambled eggs and coffee, which, rather to her own surprise, she attacked with gusto; it gave her something to do as she recounted the proposal Greg had put to her and her own naïveté in trusting him to carry through his side of the bargain. 'So at the end of this month Keith Hastings will be the owner of Marshwinds,' she finished, picking up a lump of sugar with chased silver tongs and dropping it into her coffee. 'It's the only home Ross has ever known, Rowena. And he's going to lose it!'

Rowena's eyes were bright with interest, her hair an aureole that seemed to crackle with its own energy. 'Keith Hastings is a most unsavoury character,' she said primly. 'I maintain a number of close contacts with the province's business community; he does not have a reputation for probity. It would be a most unfortunate occurrence for him to purchase Marshwinds—I am totally opposed to the splitting up of our agricultural land into subdivisions. Something must be done.'

Sharon took a long sip of coffee, feeling infinitely better for having shared her dilemma with Rowena; her own mother, she recognised with a touch of sadness, would not have welcomed these disclosures, nor offered the support of either attention or action: Sharon had been the strong one in that relationship.

'Greg Bowen . . .' Rowena mused out loud. 'He's with the firm of Broadstairs, Hart and Bowen, isn't he?'

Sharon frowned. 'I believe he is. I met Mr Broadstairs at a reception I attended with Greg a week or so ago.' She had been wearing the electric blue dress, she remembered; Arnold Broadstairs, a gentleman of the old school, had not been impressed. Even now she flushed a little as she remembered his sardonic survey of her: another of Greg's social butterflies.

'Approximately once every six months Arnold proposes to me,' said Rowena with a casualness that almost deceived Sharon. 'I should have no trouble in getting a certain—pressure, shall we say, applied to Mr Gregory Bowen. I think you will find before the day is out that Marshwinds will be offered to your Ross at the lowest possible price. After all, if the story of Greg's little scheme were to get out, it could only harm him. Halifax is too small a community for him to do that kind of thing with impunity; he does have to maintain a certain image, I'm sure you can see that.'

'That's blackmail, Rowena!'

'You fight fire with fire, dear. To make sure there are absolutely no last-minute hitches, I shall lend your Ross the entire purchase price. I'll give you a cheque. He and I can work out terms of payment.'

'Rowena . . .' The tears could not be blinked back this time. Sharon added childishly, 'He's not my Ross.'

'Then it's high time he was. Now, if you'll excuse me for a few minutes, I shall telephone Arnold.'

Ramrod-straight, Rowena stalked out of the room: a tiny, deadly frigate sailing into battle against the ponderous galleons that were Keith and Greg. Smiling mistily at her own conceit, Sharon watched her go. It would be, she sensed, a rout.

Getting up, she wandered over to the windows, gazing out over the peaceful, verdant fields. Marshwinds would belong to Ross, his for the rest of his life. For the moment that was happiness enough. . . .

In what seemed like a very short time, Rowena came

back into the room, joining the girl at the window. 'It's all settled,' she said calmly. 'I knew Arnold would understand the situation.' She paused reflectively. 'Maybe next time he asks me to marry him, I'll say yes. It's so refreshing to be with a man with brains—particularly when he has a sense of humour. Anyway, that's beside the point. Greg will be at Marshwinds at three-thirty this afternoon with all the necessary documents, I have telephoned the bank and the money will be transferred immediately, and I shall write a note to Ross, which you will give to him.' She looked her granddaughter straight in the eye. 'The rest is up to you.'

'It's up to him as well, Gran.' The last word slipped so easily from Sharon's tongue that it almost escaped the notice of both of them. But not quite. Rowena briefly squeezed Sharon's arm, her eyes filled with mute gratitude for the acknowledgment of a relationship that had been so long lost to both of them.

'Nonsense! If you can't bring the man around, you're not Elizabeth's daughter or my granddaughter.' She added firmly, 'I want to dance at your wedding, Sharon—and soon.'

'In that case, I shall expect to dance at yours as well.'

For once Rowena was at a loss. 'Enough of this nonsense. Perhaps, instead of giving you a note, I shall telephone Ross—it would be simpler, I think. And now you'd better be off. I shall come and visit you both the day after tomorrow.'

'I'll look forward to that.' Sharon added simply, 'I don't know how to thank you, Gran.'

Tartly Rowena replied, 'Marry Ross Bowen and make me a great-grandmother.'

Blushing and laughing at the same time, Sharon said, 'You make it sound so easy!'

'I only met him the once, Sharon, but it was enough to convince me he's the right one for you. One doesn't often meet that combination of strength and integrity.' A twinkle appeared in Rowena's eyes. 'If I were forty years younger, you'd have a serious rival—I always did have a weakness for blue eyes.'

'You're hopeless! I'd better go—and Gran, thanks.'

'A pleasure, my dear.' And there was no doubt in Sharon's mind that Rowena meant that quite literally.

The drive home was uneventful. At the top of the hill that overlooked the farm, Sharon stopped the car and got out for a minute. The buildings were dwarfed by distance, the orchards reduced to long, straight rows that curved sinuously over the hillside. The dykeland drowsed in the sunshine, edged by the hard blue gleam of the sea. It was incredibly beautiful, and, after today, it would belong to Ross.

For the first time it occurred to her to wonder whether he would be grateful to her for what was, essentially, a meddling in his affairs. Perhaps he would resent the fact that it was she who had secured Marshwinds for him; he did, after all, despise her for her liason with Greg. Would she be staying on at the farm? Or would he want to leave at the end of the month anyway?

Her pleasure in the scene before her evaporated. It was all very well for Rowena to say blithely that Ross was the man for Sharon; if Ross didn't think so, no amount of positive thinking on Rowena's part would help the situation. Slowly Sharon got back in the car and eased it into gear.

When she arrived at the farm and went into the kitchen, Jock was loading plates into the dishwasher. He nodded at her, a quizzical look on his grizzled face. 'Afternoon, miss. There's cold meat and salad in the refrigerator for you.'

She put the keys back on the shelf, suddenly feeling very tired. 'I don't think I'm hungry, Jock. Where's Ross?'

'Gone to the bank.' He paused delicately. 'He looked a different man, if I may say so.'

Because he had Marshwinds, that was why he was happy, she thought numbly. 'That's good . . . I'd better get changed, and take some alfalfa down to the pasture.'

She trailed to her room and changed into jeans and a pale blue knit shirt, looping her hair into two pigtails.

In the lofty-ceilinged barn the swallows flew in and out, watched from below by the yellow-eyed cats. Otherwise it was silent and still. Sharon went outside and got the truck, backing it up by the door, then began to lug the bales of alfalfa from the barn to the truck, heaping them loosely; a dozen should be enough. She was bending to get the last one when a voice spoke behind her. Prosaically enough all it said was, 'Oh, so here you are.' But there was an undertone of menace that brought her instantly upright. Letting go of the bale, she turned, knowing whom she was going to see.

'Hello, Greg,' she said emotionlessly.

He walked further into the barn, his highly polished leather shoes sounding very loud on the uneven boards. Earlier the utter silence of the barn had made of it a haven; now it merely emphasised Sharon's aloneness. She had seen Greg in many moods: jocular, businesslike, amatory, vengeful. But she had never seen such banked-up fury and frustration as there was in him now. Instinctively she stepped back a pace, only to have him come two steps closer. He said something so obscene that she blanched.

Collecting herself, she said coldly, 'It's Ross you want to see, not me.'

'Ross's car was parked by the bank when I came through town. I came early on purpose, in order to congratulate you in person.'

For a crazy moment she thought of Rowena and all the talk of weddings. 'What for?' she replied faintly.

Another step closer. 'Why, on getting the better of me. What else? Very clever of you to apply pressure via Arnold.'

There was no point in evading the issue. Sharon said tersely, 'If you'd kept your side of the bargain, I wouldn't have had to do that.'

'You little bitch! I wanted to take over that firm eventually—you've certainly ruined any chance I had of doing that.'

Unwisely she retorted, 'Perhaps that'll teach you to keep your word.'

His smile was an ugly stretching of his lips, not

reaching his eyes. 'It's a bit late for that, isn't it? As I'm finished anyway, Sharon, I figure I might as well reap some of the benefits. You and I gave a pretty good approximation of being lovers. Now we're going to make it a reality.'

His lunge was so unexpectedly swift that she failed to duck in time. He had pulled her close to his body and his face was only inches from hers before, belatedly, she began to struggle. 'Don't be silly, Greg!' she gasped. 'You know you won't get away with it.'

'We'll be the only ones to know it's the first time. I won't tell—and who do you think will believe you?'

He meant every word he was saying, and there was, of course, the distinct possibility that he was right: who would believe her? Fear closed her throat. Her eyes dilated. Frantically she kicked out at him, flinging her weight forwards and then backwards in an effort to loosen his hold.

She had reckoned without his determination or his strength. Neatly he hooked his leg around hers, pulling her feet out from under her so that she lost her balance and toppled back into the hay. Then he was on top of her, his weight suffocating her, one hand bruising her breast even as the other pinned down her flailing arms. She gathered her breath to scream, twisting her neck to avoid his kiss. But he grabbed her chin, forcing her head back, and for a terrifying instant of helplessness, she knew there was nothing she could do to stop him. Her cry was bitten off as his mouth seized hers. Spots danced in front of her eyes. Revulsion and panic giving her a strength she did not know she possessed, she lashed out with her legs, only to have them pinioned beneath his thighs. Trapped, scarcely able to breathe, she felt her head begin to spin.

Then, from one moment to the next, like a sequence in a dream, she was lying alone in the hay. The weight was gone, torn from her. She could breathe again. Hearing an ugly thud, flesh on flesh, she opened her eyes. The tableau was one she never forgot.

Unheard by either her or Greg, Ross had entered the barn: it must have been he who had bodily hauled Greg off her. The sound she had heard, she realised, pushing herself up on one elbow, had been Ross's fist connecting with Greg's jaw, for there was a trickle of blood running from the corner of Greg's mouth. Ross had him pinned against the wall. The note in his voice was one she had never heard before: murderously low, absolutely sincere. 'I could kill you for what you were doing to Sharon,' he rasped. 'You know that, don't you? You'd better believe it, Greg, because if I ever catch you within ten feet of her again, I'll hit out first and ask questions afterwards. Have you got that straight?'

Greg looked terrified, as well he might, his normally ruddy complexion a sickly grey. But even then he tried to lie his way out of it. 'I wasn't doing anything I hadn't done before,' he croaked. 'Just ask——'

Mercilessly Ross tightened his hold on Greg's collar, so that Greg's stumbled explanation was cut off in an ignominious croak. 'You're lying,' Ross said deliberately. 'I heard you as I was coming in the door. Your so-called affair with Sharon was nothing but an act. A very good act, mind you—it sure as hell had me convinced. But an act, nevertheless.' In sudden disgust he dropped his hands to his sides, stepping back; Greg sagged against the wall, his tie askew, his normally sleek hair rumpled. Ross said contemptuously, 'Go on over to the house. Let's get those papers signed and the deal closed. Then I want you off my land and out of my life, Greg—Marshwinds isn't big enough for both of us. Go on. I'll follow in a minute.'

Trying very hard to gather some semblance of dignity, but succeeding in merely looking shifty, Greg stumbled across the barn floor and out of the door. Not until he was gone did Sharon release her breath in a long sigh. Now that the threat was removed, she discovered she was trembling. Eyes still dazed with shock, she waited for whatever Ross would do next.

He knelt beside her in the hay. 'Did he hurt you?'

'No, it's okay. He scared me, that's all.'

'The bastard.'

For all the quietness of Ross's voice, Sharon shivered. 'I'm glad you came when you did.'

'I should have interrupted sooner. It took me a minute to take in what he was saying—that it had all been an act.' He squeezed her shoulder gently. 'Look, why don't you stay here? It'll only take a few minutes for Greg and me to finish our business, and then I'll come back here.' He smoothed her hair back from her forehead, and at the look of undisguised tenderness on his face, a new trembling began that was not fear.

She said submissively, lacking both the energy and the will to argue, 'All right.'

His lips brushed her cheek and a deep, instinctive happiness welled up within her. Violet-blue, her eyes glowed shyly. 'Sharon, I don't——' Ross broke off, straightening slowly. 'We'll talk later. I need to get Greg out of the way first. I won't be long.'

She watched him leave, allowing herself to admire the long straight line of his back, the lithe, almost animal-like, grace of his walk. She should finish the alfalfa, she supposed ... but she was still shaken from the encounter with Greg, forcing to the back of her mind the memory of his rough, fumbling hands and brutal strength. After today, he would have no more reason to come to Marshwinds, thank goodness. Following her train of thought, she realised she was going on the assumption that she herself would remain here. Would she? Even if Ross did believe her innocent of any real involvement with Greg, it did not necessarily follow that he wanted any further involvement with her himself.

She lay back on the hay, too tired to think about it anymore. Whether she stayed or whether she left, she thought fuzzily, she would at least have the satisfaction of knowing Ross did not think her a cheap little tramp who had slept with a man he despised; it was a strangely comforting thought. Her head fell back on the hay. It was soft and dry, and the peace of the old barn, disrupted by Greg's intrusive presence, reasserted itself. The swallows chittered softly to themselves. The dust particles floated gently downwards, bright specks in the beams of sunlight slanting from the high windows. It had been a long day and she was tired . . . her eyes shut and within a few minutes she was fast asleep.

Half an hour later Ross came back into the barn. He hesitated in the doorway, his eyes adjusting to the gloom. Then he saw the girl and walked forward, his footsteps soundless.

Sharon was lying on her back, her cheek cradled in one hand, her hair a sleek, iridescent black against the dusty hay. Her eyelids under the straight black brows were brushed with mauve shadows, as though the violet of her irises was glowing through. Her breast rose and fell gently with the rhythm of her breathing.

He stood there for several minutes watching her, his expression unreadable. Whether he was remembering another time, a wet, stormy night when he had found a girl sleeping in his barn, there was no way of telling. Then he knelt at her side, raising the hand that lay, palm up, to his lips.

Sharon woke very gradually, moving from the vague recollection of a dream about Ross to the dreamlike reality of lips warm against her hand. She smiled at him sleepily. 'Has he gone?' she asked.

There was no need for her to specify whom she meant. 'Yes, he's gone. And he won't be back.' His smile was exultant. 'Marshwinds is mine, Sharon. Legally, irrevocably, mine!'

Only now could she admit to herself that she had been afraid of some last-minute hitch that would mean that Greg, after all, had been the winner. She sat up, resting a hand on Ross's bare forearm. 'I'm so pleased,' she said simply. 'It means the world to you, doesn't it?'

'Yes.'

A tiny monosyllable, yet it seemed to say to Sharon all that she had many times suspected: Marshwinds was paramount in Ross's life, far more important to him than any woman could ever be. Her long, thick lashes flickered down to hide her eyes. 'You can plan ahead now, make all the improvements you want to, and know that it's totally yours,' she murmured. 'It must make such a difference to know that.'

'Look at me, Sharon.'

Unwillingly she glanced up. He said quietly, 'Of course it makes a difference. It means I'm not going to be torn up by the roots, that I'm going to benefit from all the years of work I've poured into the place. I don't know how to begin to thank you, Sharon. If it wasn't for you and your grandmother, I'd have been thrown out of here in three more days.'

'It was my grandmother's doing,' she disclaimed hastily. 'She's the one who knew Arnold Broadstairs, and she's the one with the money.'

'But you're the one who went and asked her. And you're the one who put up with Greg's attentions because you thought that way you'd save the farm for me.'

She looked at him uncertainly. 'How do you know that?'

'Your grandmother told me as much.' His eyes glinted mischievously. 'She's quite a lady, your grandmother. Because she also told me in no uncertain terms that if I'd believed you were infatuated with Greg, I really didn't deserve to win you in the end.'

'Oh!' Sharon stared at him blankly, a blush creeping up her cheeks. Searching for something to say, she added hurriedly, 'Greg cheated, though. He'd never intended letting you have the place at all.'

'Of course not,' Ross responded grimly. 'You're far too trusting, Sharon—whereas I haven't been trusting enough.' He was still holding her hand, and gazed down at her slim, tanned fingers as though he'd never seen them before, or as if he was committing every detail of them to memory. 'First of all, because of Peter, I had you labelled as some kind of promiscuous drug addict. As I grew to know you, I realised that was a totally false picture, that you were honest and brave and true. And then Greg came along. . . .' He paused, absently rubbing the oval of her fingernail with the ball of his finger. 'I reacted so violently because it *was* Greg,' he said finally. 'That's the only excuse I can offer. You know through the years I tried to be a real brother to him, even to be his friend—but it was impossible. He came to stand for everything I hate: the amassing of money for the power it entails, the total disrespect for the environment, the ruthless use of people as pawns in a financial game that's essentially immoral. Oh, I could go on and on. So when I saw you and him together, I saw red. The only way I could handle it was to withdraw. Far from the best way to deal with it, I'm sure.' He grinned crookedly. 'A good bit of it was plain, old-fashioned jealousy, too. I couldn't bear to think of the two of you together, of him kissing you and touching you.' Unconsciously his fingers tightened on hers.

'You're hurting,' she said mildly, while inwardly her heart was beating an erratic refrain. Jealous? Why would Ross be jealous?

Perhaps the question had shown in her face. He said evenly, 'I wanted you for myself, you see. After that day on the beach, you must have realised that.'

'Yes. . . .' It took every ounce of her courage to ask the all-important question, 'Why do you want me, Ross? What's so special about me?'

He laughed indulgently. 'Come on, Sharon, you must know the answer to that!'

Her eyes flashed. 'If I did, I wouldn't be asking.'

As if he could not help himself, he drew her close to his chest, burying his face in the fragrant fall of her hair. 'You've just given me one of the reasons—because you're full of spirit. You won't let me—or any of our children—away with anything, will you, sweetheart? Oh, Sharon, don't you know what I'm saying? I'm saying I love you. That I fell in love with you that first night when I found you here with your drenched black hair and your big purple eyes. But I fought it all the way. How could a girl whose waist I could span turn my world upside down? A girl from nowhere, with a past she refused to talk about?' He trailed kisses down the slender length of her neck. 'That's what I told myself. But it didn't make any difference. I just fell more and more deeply in love with you with every minute I spent in your company.' Abruptly he raised his head, his blue eyes anxious. 'You're not saying a word.

Sharon, maybe you don't love me now, but I'm willing to wait. Heaven help me, I'll wait for ten years if that's what it takes. Because I know you're the only woman in the world I want to marry. I want to live with you until the day I die. And I want you to be the mother of my children.'

It was her turn to draw him close. With an entrancing mixture of shyness and boldness, she raised her face for his kiss. It was a kiss that said without words all that was in her heart; when they finally moved apart, she said softly, the simple words a pledge, 'I love you, Ross. How could I not? You're all I've ever wanted or will ever want.'

As though his body could express what words could not, he drew her down into the hay, raining kisses on her face and lips, his hands urgent in their demand; her hunger for him was every bit as fierce and elemental as his for her. Yet, in a kind of mutual understanding, something held them back. It was Ross who put it into words. 'I want you, Sharon.' He drew her palm to his chest where his heartbeat thudded against his ribcage. 'I want to make you mine, never doubt that. But——' His eyes crinkled with laughter, 'provided you'll marry me as soon as it's humanly possible, I'd rather wait until we're married. Can you understand that?'

'Of course I can.' Sharon ran her finger along the width of his mouth, delighting in her freedom to touch him; the security of their newly discovered love had given her that, and had moreover, enabled her to sense the pleasure he gained from her shy caresses. 'I'd rather wait, too,' she said. 'I guess I'm basically old-fashioned, Ross. I'd like to wear a long white dress and to know it symbolises the gift not only of my body but of my whole being as I come into your care.'

'I knew you'd understand, sweetheart. And I promise with all my heart to care for you and love you until the end of my days.'

Her eyes shining with happiness, she cupped his face in her hands and kissed him gently, full on the lips. 'I promise the same.'

From outside the barn, exaggeratedly loud, came the

scrape of footsteps. A throat was cleared equally loudly. 'Ross? Are you there, sir?'

Ross sat up, his face alight with laughter. 'It's quite safe to come in, Jock. Sharon, you've got hay in your hair. Disgraceful, eh, Jock?'

'I couldn't say, sir.'

'You're not that old, Jock! By the way, be the first to congratulate us. I've finally persuaded Sharon to marry me—took me long enough, didn't it?'

'I *was* beginning to wonder,' Jock replied decorously. 'Congratualtions, miss. You've got yourself a fine man.'

'I know it, Jock.'

Ross ran his fingers through his own hair, pulling out stalks of hay with overdone surprise. 'How did they get there? Jock, you must have had a reason for coming here. Other than to chaperone, that is.'

'Aye, sir. Doug says an axle's broken on the green tractor, and that the cows have got through the fence up by the orchard.'

'Damn!' Ross grinned ruefully at Sharon. 'We'd better go. This'll probably be the story of our life, Sharon—there always seems to be some kind of a crisis on a farm. Will you mind?'

'Not as long as you're the one to round up Myrtle!' she responded, chuckling. She scrambled to her feet and reached down a hand to help him up. 'Let's go.'

He kept her hand in his and together they walked out of the barn into the sunshine, where the rolling green acres of Marshwinds waited for them.

Harlequin® Plus

A WORD ABOUT THE AUTHOR

Born in England, Sandra Field today makes her home in Nova Scotia, Canada. Converts, she says, are usually fanatical in their new beliefs, and Sandra is strongly attached to the Maritimes, with its sometimes inhospitable climate but breathtakingly beautiful scenery.

She has lived in all three of Canada's Maritime provinces, but it was during her stay on tiny Prince Edward Island, where the beaches are legendary but the winters long, that she decided to write a book. The local library provided her with a guide for aspiring authors, and she followed the instructions to a "t."

It was no simple job, she recalls now. In fact, a major crisis occured when she ran out of plot several thousand words short of the mark! But a good friend coaxed her into completing the manuscript for the simple reason that she wanted to read it. The book was *To Trust My Love* (Romance #1870), published in 1975.

Her many interests, which she likes to weave into her stories, include birdwatching, studying wild flowers and participating in such winter activities as snowshoeing and cross-country skiing. She particularly enjoys classical music, especially that of the Romantic period.

Take these 4 best-selling novels FREE

Get this book FREE!

Mail to:
Harlequin Reader Service

In the U.S.
2504 West Southern Avenue
Tempe, AZ 85282

In Canada
649 Ontario Street
Stratford, Ontario N5A 6W2

YES! I want to be one of the first to discover **Harlequin American Romance.** Send me FREE and without obligation *Twice in a Lifetime.* If you do not hear from me after I have examined my FREE book, please send me the 4 new **Harlequin American Romances** each month as soon as they come off the presses. I understand that I will be billed only $2.25 for each book (total $9.00). There are no shipping or handling charges. There is no minimum number of books that I have to purchase. In fact, I may cancel this arrangement at any time. *Twice in a Lifetime* is mine to keep as a FREE gift, even if I do not buy any additional books.

Name _____ (please print)

Address _____ Apt. no. _____

City _____ State/Prov. _____ Zip/Postal Code _____

Signature (If under 18, parent or guardian must sign.)

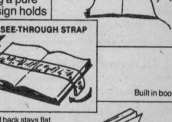